EAST RENFREWSHIRE

KT-370-028

Praise for Heinz Helle's *Superabundance*

'[A] philosophical tour de force ... which aptly showcases Helle's deadpan humour. This is a linguistically daring portrait of an overwhelmed mind' *Financial Times*

'Fragmentary prose is welded by a hypnotic voice ... the unnamed narrator of Heinz Helle's debut describes his life in New York with remorseless logic' *Guardian*

'Beckettian ... excellent ... funny' *Independent*

'Darkly humorous ... Helle shows us the world with a rare clear-sightedness' *Scotland on Sunday*

'A work of deadpan brilliance and unflinching honesty, chasing down lines of thought normally lost in the cacophony of our daily lives. I had always assumed I was fully conscious until I read this' Alex Christofi, author of *Glass*

'A nearly flawless, driving history of total alienation' *Die Zeit*

'So modern, so cool, so strange' Hubert Winkels

EUPHORIA

HEINZ HELLE

translated by Kári Driscoll

With the support of the Swiss Arts Council Pro Helvetia

First published in Great Britain in 2017 by Serpent's Tail,
an imprint of Profile Books Ltd
3 Holford Yard
Bevin Way
London WC1X 9HD
www.serpentstail.com

Euphoria was first published as *Eigentlich müssten wir tanzen* by
Suhrkamp Verlag Berlin in 2015
Copyright © 2015 by Heinz Helle
Translation copyright © 2017 Kári Driscoll

1 3 5 7 9 10 8 6 4 2

Designed and typeset by sue@lambledesign.demon.co.uk
Printed and bound by CPI Group (UK) Ltd, Croydon CR0 4YY

The moral right of the author has been asserted.

All rights reserved. Without limiting the rights under copyright
reserved above, no part of this publication may be reproduced,
stored or introduced into a retrieval system, or transmitted, in
any form or by any means (electronic, mechanical, photocopying,
recording or otherwise), without the prior written permission of
both the copyright owner and the publisher of this book.

The characters and events in this book are fictitious.
Any similarity to real persons, dead or alive, is coincidental and
not intended by the author

A CIP record for this book can be obtained from the British Library

ISBN 978 1 78125 688 6
eISBN 978 1 78283 277 5

FSC
www.fsc.org

MIX
Paper from
responsible sources
FSC® C018072

for Chris

I stood on the shore and talked to the surf BLABLA,
behind me the ruins of Europe.

Heiner Müller

I'm only doing this because I want to go to Heaven.

Sido

1 When it's too cold to lie down at night we remain standing. We stand close together, back to back to side to front. We turn slowly over the course of the night so that each of us gets a turn in the middle, and from time to time each one of us has to be on the outside. When the sun comes up we look past each other, avoiding eye contact, and we can clearly see out of the corners of our eyes that the others are also looking in some other direction. Each of us is looking somewhere else, each into his own distant nothing, or everything, it doesn't matter, we don't look each other in the eye, that would be painful, a different and far greater pain than looking at the sun as it rises. Usually it's cloudy, and we continue to look past each other and feel relief at the receding cold and the increasing light and we stand huddled together, almost like we did before, on the underground, at rush hour.

2 In the twilight we see a kid. It is sitting a little away from the road, which isn't really a road so much as a path, and it is sitting upright and casually and introverted, facing the charred remains of a tent, which it is hitting at regular intervals with a rotten branch. We stop. Strangely, the form and circumstance of the child's body do not trigger any protective impulse in us, nor any emotion or warmth. We look at the kid, see the thin hair on the back of his head, the too-short neck, the short, soft limbs carrying out violent, senseless movements with great seriousness and concentration, as if this were some sort of scientific experiment involving hitting sheets of nylon repeatedly with a charred piece of wood. The kid still looks quite well fed. He will last another week at least, assuming it doesn't suddenly turn colder. Maybe his mother is just off fetching water or something. We leave him alone. As we start moving

again the kid turns around and stares at us. I'm afraid he will start crying because I don't know what we would do to get him to stop. But he just sizes us up, one after the other, his face totally expressionless. Then he turns to face the burnt-out collapsed tent and hits it with his charred stick again: smack, smack, smack. We move on. After a little while we find his parents, lying in the bushes with their skulls smashed open.

3 The next day it's darker and a light drizzle sets in, growing imperceptibly denser and denser. It is as if it's not droplets of water that are falling on us, on the black tar and on the gravel crunching beneath our feet, but rather fine, unbroken streams, like the trickle of a thousand leaky taps. The type of rain whose intensity you don't notice until you are soaked through, and you stop and look down at yourself and then up at the sky and shake your head in disbelief.

We get off the road. We walk through brown fields, traverse gentle hills, meadows and other open spaces whose function is unclear. Ahead of us is a gigantic, flat block. We walk towards it. It takes longer than we thought. It's farther away than we thought. It is much, much bigger than we thought. The exterior walls are over thirty feet tall and punctuated by sliding doors of rusty steel and broken glass. Chimneys. A former factory, perhaps. As we circle the bare, angular cube in search of a way in, the rain gets heavier and the sound of the drops on the building's roof is tinny and bright, it gets louder and less fragmentary and soon the building is transformed into one big resonance chamber, singing a single, high-pitched note.

We find a door frame. The door is gone. We go in, one after the other, and oddly the sound of the rain on the roof is barely audible on the inside. We are in a big, empty hall. The floor is littered with broken glass, abandoned campfires, it smells of old oil, and there are stains left behind by various substances that have seeped into the concrete. The assembly pits reveal that this used to be a place for servicing cars or farming machines. Apart from the stains, the floor, the walls, and the roof on which the rain is falling, there is nothing here. We leave the building and walk on, through the dense rainfall, back to the forest.

4 In the last light we reach a village. Here too all the windows are shuttered, the doors bolted. We encounter no one and find no indication of the inhabitants' whereabouts. We go into a supermarket through the broken glass door. We walk up and down rows of empty and half-empty shelves. The floor is strewn with torn packaging, broken glass, dented aluminium and squashed cardboard boxes, and everything is shrouded in the inevitable, almost unbearable smell: the smell of all the things that were ever in a supermarket. Packaged soups, crisps, chocolate, cat food, drain cleaner, frozen lasagne, deodorant, beer, rotting meat. We find a pallet of water bottles and a couple of sticks of garlic bread still in their plastic packaging. With our bounty we withdraw into the warmest and safest room of the abandoned complex: the defrosted cold storage room. We eat, we drink, we sit in silence. It's a good silence, a kind of,

See, it's not so bad, we can make it, we'll find a way. And we savour the cold garlic bread. The butter tastes good when it's this hard, you really have to bite it in order to taste the intense flavour. After the exertion of the past few days, the fat is like a revelation. Having made sure we can't be locked in from the outside, we build a camp out of alternating layers of cardboard and plastic wrapping. We lie down side by side and then we cover ourselves with more layers of cardboard, resting our heads on wads of plastic, the bottles of mineral water within reach. Our breathing doesn't just sound exhausted. It sounds peaceful.

5 A few weeks ago we were in the car. The autobahn was mostly empty, and on either side the grey-green alpine upland was covered in a thin layer of frost. The hard shoulder was covered in gravel and the dirt of weeks past. Another age. And the radio was playing a song that we all claimed not to know and never to have heard before, but now we were all roaring the chorus:

Euphoria!

Forever till the end of time

From now on, only you and I

We were flying up the Irschenberg – in actual fact we were driving, of course, but you always fly up the Irschenberg, never down it. The difference between coming and going is categorical. We were going fast, the noise of the revving engine sounded like courage and determination. To our right groaning lorries, creeping, crawling up the hill: pathetic beasts, fused with their drivers. A docile herd caught in the daily to and fro of the working week, which, to us, ever since we got in the car, had seemed as distant, harmless and controllable as death.

There were five of us. Drygalski, Gruber, Fürst, Golde, and me. We had packed eggs and milk, beer, mince, pasta, Nutella, everything except for bread, which we wanted to buy at the baker's in the village, down in the valley. We had left the city behind us, the suburb where we had grown up together, the autobahn junctions, the carpet, furniture and DIY stores, the industrial estates that were home to companies with metal detectors and security guards and complicated English names that had something to do with computers. Two in the front, three in the back. We were packed in tight. The ones in the back could have held hands if they had wanted to, but that would have been gay, and in any case, notwithstanding the euphoria we felt at our communal forward motion, we also felt a certain distance from one another; after all, it would never be as much fun as it used to be, just more expensive each year, and really we were all getting too old for this stuff, and besides it now took us at least three days to recover from a decent bender.

On the crest of the Irschenberg, just as we saw the golden arches, one of us shouted, McFlurry!, and another one of us laughed, though the one driving just gave a tired smile and raced on, past the American fast food restaurant whose menu we had known off by heart before we had even learnt to play cards, if we ever even had, and then we drove steeply downhill. Through the windscreen we saw the Inn valley spread out before us, dark green, empty and silent, all the way to the misty Alps, dissected by six straight lanes of civilisation, trailing on in shimmering red and white. The windscreen wipers squeaked.

6   The following morning we leave the village on foot and take the highway that runs the length of the valley. It takes us around the next mountain, through the next valley, past the next mountain. We pass signs with the names of towns that are probably deserted now, and no sooner have we passed them than we've forgotten them again. We see pylons with no wires between them, abandoned petrol stations, super-markets, holiday homes, vacancy signs, here and there the burnt-out wreck of a car.

We get to a lake. The opposite shore is out of sight; this one is full of charred sailing boats, smashed furniture and bottles, empty packaging and articles of clothing. Bloated corpses. As if anything went away just because you throw it in the water. The only dissolution in sight is the way the gentle waves merge with the low-hanging grey clouds. We've quickly seen enough and turn away, towards the small town on the lake shore, the small town presumably built here for the fantastic view it provides of the lake on clear days. We head for the promenade. We walk across the gravel, past the debris, to the street and up the steps to a hotel. We cross a terrace strewn with uprooted parasols, tables and chairs. We walk through the open double doors into the deserted dining hall. Under a heap of dishes in the filthy kitchen we find an unopened bottle of condensed milk. The oily liquid leaves a film behind in our throats. The taste is irrelevant. We tell ourselves that it's filling.

At the other end of town, in a cluster of low-rise buildings which, according to the adjacent sign, was once the industrial estate, we find an abandoned bowling alley. We walk down the steps, not knowing why, we just keep going. A dull grey falls on the lanes from the skylights overhead. There is no electricity. The bowling pins are gone, perhaps they're in the pin setter, in any case we can't see them. After a few minutes' indecision, our eyes fall on the heavy balls with the three holes lying next to the lanes, dusty and detached, somehow completely normal. So we pick up one after the other and send them barrelling down the empty lanes into the darkness. We listen to them rolling along until they produce a dull thud in the inaccessible padded space behind where the target used to be.

7 In the grey light between the denuded trees the tarmac quickly starts to crack, pushed up by the roots, pushed down by heavy forestry machines. A few minutes later the road surface disintegrates completely, turns to gravel. The gravel thins out; the road becomes a path, the path becomes a track, and the track becomes open ground. I wonder if it's just the road that is disappearing or if it's everything, and whether you couldn't see it as liberating not to have anything telling you which way to go, apart from the trees, wet and black, that emerge at regular intervals from the fog before disappearing behind us again. We avoid them. It is easy and advisable, but otherwise there is nothing to decide or to discuss about which direction we should go in. After a couple of hours we spot something to our right that doesn't belong here. It isn't dark, and it isn't sticking vertically up out of the ground, or lying

flat on it, or leaning against one of the other vertical, dark, wooden pillars of this sylvan world order. It is lying there contorted and spastic, seemingly thrown there. The trees around it are strangely splintered, strangely because the jagged splinters that remain after a branch has broken off usually aren't as black and edgeless as the damp, soft bark. The thing has a round, heavily dented body and a long, thin tail with a fin or a flag at the end, and the thing is yellow, yellower than anything we've seen in weeks. We see the bent rotor blades, sticking out at crazy angles, like broken arms and legs. We see the dried blood from the pilot's body, which is hanging halfway out of the cockpit. We see the smashed glass of the fuselage, the circle of stars on the blue rectangle on the tailfin. And then we see the four large, black letters on the side of the fuselage. And we find it hard to imagine that such people really existed, not too long ago, who would fly through the air observing the traffic conditions on the autobahns in Bavaria and Tyrol.

We search through the wreckage for anything we can use, then we search the bodies. We find a first aid kit, a toolbox, and a manual with international radio codes, but the radio is built-in and broken and none of us is tech-savvy enough to be able to get it out and repair it, so we leave the manual behind and move on. After an hour no one wants to carry the heavy toolbox any more so we leave it in the forest, and two hours later we abandon the first aid kit as well, and we trudge on through our steaming breath and the drizzle and think about the two pilots' padded uniforms, and their boots and vests, and about how it's all soaked in blood and rain, and that the only thing from the crash site that we've still got is the hammer from the toolbox, and the one carrying that hammer is me.

8 Just a few weeks ago I was in the air. I was completing step fifty-seven of a clearly defined fifty-eight step workflow for the eight hundred and ninety-sixth time, five hundred of which were during my training, four hundred and fifty in the simulator, fifty in the real world, so to speak, somewhere in the Arizona desert, where, together with two instructors from a major German airline, in an otherwise empty Boeing 737, ten times a day, for five days straight, I took off, flew around in a circle, landed, took off, flew in a circle, landed, and so on.

I was flying direct from Mauritius to Frankfurt and I had a little over eleven hours to remind myself that this was the profession I had wanted ever since I knew what a profession was. I was a pilot. The plane was fully booked. There were two hundred and twenty-nine people on board, about whom I knew only two things for certain: they had taken off with me from Mauritius, and they wanted to land with me in Frankfurt. Unusually for me, I was trying to imagine the view from the open cockpit door, the view behind me, before take-off, before the first class curtains were drawn. I saw heads, each covering portions of the white antimacassars on the headrests. I saw hair. The hair was of all different colours: blond, black, white, grey, red or green or blue. Anyone could fly so long as they bought a ticket and had a passport. I saw ears. Big ears and small ears, hairy ears, round ears, wizened and stunted ears, sticky-out ears, and perfectly ordinary ears. I saw eyes. They were brown, green, black, blue, and they were not all looking straight ahead, in my direction, they were looking out of the window, at the newspaper in front of them, they were staring in silence at the tray table, which was stowed for take-off. I couldn't see what they were wearing, but I knew they were wearing clothes of all conceivable colours and cuts, in all price ranges, in all styles and fabrics: jeans, suits, shorts, ribbed undershirts, viscose rayon underwear, cotton socks, nylon stockings, leather shoes, rubber running shoes, Birkenstock sandals. I sipped my coffee.

I tried to imagine two hundred and twenty-nine hearts. I could feel my own heart beating.

I glanced at the instrument panel and carried out step fifty-eight: the pilot switches to autopilot. We had reached cruising altitude.

9 We are standing by a small artificial lake. The water looks green and blue and completely unnatural, and in the thick reeds on the shore you can see the traces of the farming machines they've pushed into the water. A tractor, a combine harvester, a cattle truck carrying cows or pigs or lambs – between the thick bars you can make out legs and heads there underwater, or bodies in any case, something, we don't know what, but I think: animals. It is an animal transport after all. The silence is broken by a splashing, quiet but distinct, and out of the corner of my eye I can see what has landed in the water, and then I hear Drygalski's voice: Have you lost your mind? he shouts, but Gruber just shrugs his shoulders.

The rest of us reach into our trouser pockets and feel the familiar piece of plastic, with or without chrome plating, safe in our hands. Just knowing that it is there, with the hundreds of numbers, names, addresses and appointments, the personalised ringtones, the photos, the movies. We are each carrying scale models of our lives in our pockets, and even if we will never be able to return to those lives it is reassuring to have something to remember them by, something we can touch and hold and look at. The displays are black. Gruber looks serious and methodical as he pulls the charger out of his pocket as well. He looks down; the plug is stuck. He uses both hands. Between his eyes a small, vertical crease appears. He is not angry, he is concentrating. Then, with a sudden jerk of his hand, the charging cable traces an elliptical trajectory through the air. Like a helicopter that is about to crash, I think. The rubber-coated wire orbits the two prongs and the converter, until the whole thing lands not far from where the phone disappeared below the surface just a few seconds before. Gruber looks satisfied. He is standing slightly hunched over, hands in his jacket pockets, his chin thrust forward, his shoulders sagging. Like someone who would really like to be a little bit taller, just not right now. From the spot where his

Samsung smartphone with SVoice and ChatOn and all that has vanished into the water, a series of concentric circles are spreading.

10 We walk through leaves. We walk on gravel. We walk on shiny tarmac, on broken glass, shreds of rubber, metal, leather, fabric, plastic. We walk on oil. We walk on water. The puddles look like tar on the tarmac in the low evening sun. We are five different bodies, all with different legs, arms, brains, but our communal progress along this street, this meadow, this forest floor shot through with roots, connects us. It is a stable physical connection. We are soldered together like the electrons in an atom, by spin and gravitation. We are all moving in the same direction.

For the most part Golde walks in front. Just so. Golde, who always used to say, Just so, when you said something he agreed with, with his broad nose and his no-longer-quite-so-closely-cropped hair. His tall, heavy frame moves across the left-hand lane of the A12 with the same self-confidence as when he used to skip the queue at the P1 club. Only occasionally, when a familiar name appears on a sign – Wörgl, St Johann, Jochberg, Kufstein – he seems to flinch slightly, although his gait does not change in the slightest. He keeps walking like before, but if you know a person you can tell even from behind how they feel. A tiny movement, a glance at the sky, a sigh, something so inconspicuous and normal that you realise: of course he has no idea if we're on the right track either.

Kufstein, says Golde.

The pine trees beyond the crash barrier are oddly far apart. Usually it's a single blurry, green wall. We press on. How far apart the lane markings are. How raw the tarmac.

11   The cabin was on a steep slope. It was as remote as it was old. An alpine hut from the eighteenth century. The bathroom had been added at a later date, but the living room was still heated by a wood-burning stove. The snow lay heavy on the pitched roof and on the railing at the edge of the terrace that jutted far out into the void between the slope and the mountain opposite. We rounded the final bend in the road. Huffing and puffing, we approached. We had walked on foot, made the ascent, as they say in the mountains, even though the road wasn't steep; it was a snow-covered serpentine road, through forests and fields, passable by car only in the summer months. We thought we would probably drink a lot, get drunk that is, definitely, that's how it is when you get a group of men together, and so it's not a bad thing if we get a little exercise beforehand. The key was in the shed – a draughty affair full of tools

and firewood, old skis and sleds with rusty runners. The wood was piled up to the roof, against the wall, chopped to size, dry and old, waiting to be transformed into ash and smoke. We brushed the snow off our boots and trousers and went inside. Groaning, we deposited the boxes of supplies in the corridor, the backpacks full of beer a little closer to the boiler in the pantry, lest it freeze. We stood there in our thick coats and hats and scarves, stood there in a semicircle around the old stove and waited. We were still warm from the walk up, so at first we didn't notice how cold it was inside the cabin. Gruber lit the fire immediately. The room took a long time to warm up, but our sweat-soaked bodies quickly grew cold. Bloody freezing, one of us said. Gruber blew on the fire and put another log through the bright square opening. Once it was finally going, he closed the stove door, went into the pantry and switched on the electricity. With the lights on, the room looked warmer already. We put our boots, coats, hats and scarves out in the corridor and then swarmed out, our woolly-socked feet running up the slippery wooden stairs. Men with big backpacks tripping each other up, holding onto each other, jostling each other, swearing, yelling. The beds were assigned, and such and such didn't want to share with so and so. Later we were sitting at the heavy dining table. In front of us: beer. No one said a word. Outside the window nothing but a gentle, boring grey, and I thought, perhaps a snowdrift would be good, a wall of innumerable tiny reminders of nature's hostility to life. Of the possibility of closeness between people in a safe place.

12 *Galaxy*. The dome looks almost intact, not like a galaxy so much as a UFO, but the fact that this thing with its vaulted roof, the flat-roofed annexes, the car park and the takeaway stands used to be called *Galaxy* is impossible to miss: the skeletons of gigantic letters jut out from the roof into the surrounding area, visible from far away, charred, but still typographically sound. We don't know why we're going there. It seems obvious that if anything there will only be unpleasant things to see, in there, but a nightclub always exerts a strange pull, however rural and big and provincial it may be, and we know now that it isn't the peculiar and unique combination of smells – liquor, energy drinks, beer, cigarettes, sweat and perfume – that creates that gravitational pull. This place only smells burnt. It's strange. You know instantly from the smell that something burned here, even though this is not the usual

burnt smell. We've never smelt anything like this, and yet we know: there was a fire here. The outer walls are intact. No windows on a club like this, of course, so we can't peer inside. Instead we form an orderly queue, one after the other. Of course we move on after a moment's hesitation, but the brass stanchions beside us, which were once connected by ropes, the wooden fence behind them, the little window in the heavy steel door – all of this still creates the impression of having to wait to be let in, for someone you don't know and can't see to decide that you are ready for the world on the other side of that door. The red carpet is black. The door has been barred from the outside: a bar stool has been wedged into the handles of both double doors. It is bent grotesquely out of shape, and the screws holding the door handles are loose, as if the doors had been pounded repeatedly with something heavy, or by many bodies all pushing together. I can feel the others behind me pushing. We want to get inside, and right now it's up to me. I can't open the door. My eyes scan the desolate forecourt. It's surreally empty, surreally bright, surreally quiet. I picture the two thousand people who would have fitted into this dome, the hard, monotonous beats coming out of the expensive, crystal clear speakers, the carefully carefree dancing of the provincial youth, finding the technical means to make up for their distance from the nearest city, with their subwoofers and their dancing and their fucking. I picture the beautiful bodies of the farmers' daughters, who stood to inherit the organic farm with an outbuilding for husband and child, and for whom happiness right then was some MDMA and a BMW and unprotected sex on the back seat. I picture the white skin of their faces, quivering in the lacerated beams of the strobe light, their lips and eyebrows pierced, just like their tongues, nipples and belly buttons, and for a split second I expect to see that which a moment later I never could have imagined, never would have thought possible, but am seeing all the same through the tiny window in the door, in the faint light of the cracked dome: hundreds of blackened bodies.

What do you see?
Nothing. Let's go.

13   That evening we sit huddled together. We don't make a fire, because we don't have any paper, but it's also not that cold, and in any case we're not really in the mood for fire.

Do you remember when we stole that fire extinguisher from the youth club, says Gruber.

We had been drinking Gorbatschow vodka and orange juice in the car park, and then we got loud and silly and hyped up, and when we saw the huge bouncers and the even huger members of the local biker gang we got quiet and small again.

We behaved ourselves and kept our mouths shut and waited for them to check us and give us our stamps. We stood there in the queue with the adorably made-up provincial girls, behind the wooden fences, and the girls had on figure-hugging outfits and their hair pulled back and a bit too much eyeliner. And the bouncers wore bomber jackets and earpieces and that street in Forstinning felt like Sunset Boulevard, and the youth club was the Viper Room, back then. And then we were inside and we rushed to the bar and ordered more screwdrivers, all except for Fürst, he wanted a Coke, he was on antibiotics. And then we'd already run out of money, so we took our half-empty plastic cups out onto the dance floor and stood there, not daring to dance. In front of us the girls, behind us the fire extinguisher. We didn't notice it until Fürst pushed Drygalski into it. It didn't hurt, because our coats were heaped on top of it. And he just held on. To the fire extinguisher and the coats. And just for fun, just to show how strong and clever he was, he picked it up, with the coats, and wrapped the coats around it, and then he bent over, holding the fire extinguisher in both arms like a baby, and then he shouted, I'm gonna be sick! I'm gonna be sick! Look out! Get out of the way! And the girls stopped dancing and parted like the Red Sea, then the bouncers, who parted the crowd outside, escorting us, professionally and seriously, out of the club, the one of us with the ball of coats who needed to throw up and his four-man team of chaperones, and we were still shouting, He's gonna be sick!, long after we'd made it outside, and then we ran into the car park laughing at the stupid bouncers and we ran and laughed and threw the fire extinguisher onto the tarmac, again and again, as hard as we could, from greater and greater heights. Finally Gruber climbed up on the shed for the rubbish bins, and we handed him the heavy metal cylinder, and he held it above his head like Moses with the Ten Commandments, and then the thing made amazingly little noise when it hit the ground, and it didn't even crack the smooth surface of the car park, and we came out of hiding and stood in a circle around the barely scratched fire extinguisher, and the excitement we had felt at our audacity and the anticipation of the foam quickly evaporated.

Do you remember?
Yes, we remember.

14 The next day we search the charred ruins of a petrol station for paper. Because of the extreme heat of a petrol fire, the little scraps don't burn but rather dance around high up in the smoke, and they don't fall back to earth until the fire has gone out.

A frozen section is pretty impressive, Drygalski is saying. Twenty-five micrometres. Can you imagine how many slices you can get out of a mouse tumour?

I find a scrap of paper and try to undo the knot in the plastic bag hanging from my belt. I can't do it with one hand, so I put the paper in my mouth and give Drygalski a look.

It's crazy. You've got people lying there in the cancer ward waiting for someone like me to find the right ratio of fixative to tissue. Just lying there, waiting, wondering which will be finished sooner, my specimen or their lives.

If they think it's taking too long the hospital will just order it from another lab, I say.

Yes, that's true, he says, turning a charred body over onto its back with his foot and checking to see if it's still got a wallet. In the cracked leather he finds the remains of a five-euro note. Good. Unburnt paper.

15 Whenever we pass through scrubland, we hold the branches to one side for each other. We touch the hard, sharp branches carefully until we find a handhold, and then we close our fingers around it, slowly, so we can pull back if we encounter thorns, and once our grip has closed around the branch, we push it ahead of ourselves, circling around its point of origin until the path is clear. Whoever is holding the branch remains standing until the others have gone past, and then he lets go. The branch snaps back into place, trying to grab hold of whoever was holding it, but by then we are no longer there.

16 Today we find a woman. She is covered by branches, by wet, rotting branches, probably not for warmth. We see her anyway. We see her accidentally: one of us is peeing on the bush next to her. It's a sparse bush, strange that only the lower third should have branches and leaves and hair and hands. The one who was just pissing leaves his fly open and stands there for a while. He watches her in silence, we come closer because we can see from behind that he is looking at something. When we have formed a semicircle behind him, he kneels down and touches her hair, and she doesn't scream, doesn't sob, doesn't flinch, she doesn't even close her eyes. She stares straight ahead without saying a word, without seeing what is right in front of her, she is staring intently at a space that we cannot access. Her clothes or what is left of them are tattered and torn. Openings everywhere, giving access

to the openings in her body. She starts breathing faster. We can see her white, delicate hands on the shoulders of the first one of us when he is on top of her; we see her fingers, at first weirdly splayed out, then after a while buried in the fabric of the clothes covering the man on top of her; we see her head turned to the side, her eyes, which she has now closed after all, and then we hear her voice, a single note, again and again and again, and all of that makes it impossible not to think: you know you want this too.

When it's my turn, she doesn't even raise her arms, and I am only able to finish because I can remember her hands, her hands on the back of the three men before me, and I move faster, I close my eyes and imagine her fingers clutching at a strip of cloth because that's exactly what they want, what her fingers want, to hold on, that cloth, and then I finish.

After me, it's Drygalski's turn, but he breaks it off, unsatisfied. She isn't moving at all any more. Before we move on, Fürst bends down to her once more and asks her gently if she wants to come along. She doesn't respond.

We all stand around helplessly beside her motionless body in the bed of leaves. Then he rummages in his jacket pocket and pulls out a piece of bread, breaks off a corner and lays it on her stomach. On the way from the piece of bread back to his trouser pocket his hand briefly moves in the direction of her head. Perhaps he wanted to stroke her cheek one last time. Or her hair.

17 Gruber is doing press-ups. One, two. Then he stops.

Tired, eh, says Drygalski, and Gruber looks at him blankly, as if he had remarked on the Earth's gravitational pull today, or said how we weren't getting any younger, or oh, how time goes by.

Time goes by. I don't know how that happens. I have no idea how it works, what physical process it is that causes that tilt, that teetering and falling from soon into now and then and then and then.

And then Golde says: We have to go north. And what will we do there, I think. All you see are clouds and trees. For a moment all we hear is our breathing and wet snow falling from the trees.

Golde starts walking. He steps confidently over the muddy ground covered in roots and slush. We hesitate. His steps seem a little too quick, too determined. We aren't that convinced. He didn't even look up at the sky, probably he just wants to waste time until it clears up or gets dark, and his eyes didn't look into ours for very long. He wasn't trying to convince us, he just wants to convince himself, and in order to do that he has to walk on now. Of course we follow him. When he hears our steps behind him he relaxes, the tension in his shoulders melts away, and at some point he turns around.

Come on then.

The hint of a smile crosses his sunken cheeks and dry lips. He is glad we're following him. So am I.

We get to a railway crossing. The boom is down and instinctively we stop. Drygalski takes his last cigarette out of the red box of Gauloises and lights it. His heavy, powerful hands are resting on the red-and-white steel. With no cars or drivers who need to be able to see it from a distance, the boom seems excessively colourful. One by one we come and stand beside him. He smokes, we stand, the tracks gleam with rainwater. The smoke curls upwards, and intermittently it comes streaming out of Drygalski's nose and then dissipates to nothing. We rest. It's a good last cigarette. There's no hard decision, no goodbye, no one has died. We are just standing at a railway crossing. Drygalski smokes. We wait. When he's finished, we walk around the barrier. Even though I don't expect there to be any trains using these tracks any more, I feel relieved when we're safely on the other side.

18 Fürst stops at a wooden cross at the edge of the road and looks at the candles full of rainwater. His brown hair is plastered in strands across his forehead, like ropes that have been cut.

I can't go on.
Then stay here.

One by one we walk past Fürst. Drygalski stops and stands next to him. He turns and looks at him. Fürst looks down at the ground. The rain runs down their foreheads and noses. With his right fist Drygalski wipes the water from his eyes. Then Fürst bends down and unties the laces on his heavy hiking boots. They are tightly knotted, and he has to pull hard to get them open, first the left one, then the right, and then he ties them again, first the left one, then the right, and meanwhile Drygalski stands there looking at him and when Fürst gets back up he nods and then Fürst nods too and wipes the brown strands of hair from his face. They go on.

19 Drygalski complains the least but we all know he's the one who is suffering the most. He always used to be the first to get annoyed when we were out together and the others couldn't decide where to go or what to eat or when to eat, or whether to go at all. Drygalski used to be the fat one. Surprisingly, we never teased him about it. Even at the time I didn't quite understand why. Other fatsos we encountered weren't so lucky, at school or at the youth centre, but with him it was different, maybe because he'd always been there, one of us, and he'd always been fat, so his fatness wasn't a threat to us any more, we accepted his fatness like an annoying habit, and we had annoying habits of our own, and whenever he was the last to make it, wheezing and panting, through the doors of the U-Bahn that we'd had to hold open for him, whenever he couldn't get to the pass or the striker from the other

team got away from him, whenever he would stare at our girlfriends, stealthily and obviously, out of the corner of his eye, or else at our chips, then we would talk about the weather.

20 We find an abandoned campfire at the edge of a clearing. We notice the trampled grass from a distance, see the dark black of the burnt branches, the grey of the ashes on the patchy snow and the slush and the soggy dark green field. We can tell that Drygalski is getting nervous by the simple fact that he is controlling himself so much and showing the least emotion of all of us.

Do you think there's anything left?

Fürst can't control himself as easily. He nervously chews his thin lips. No reply. We move closer. Then we are standing around the ashes and the blackened wood, breathing, not looking each other in the eye, just at the ashes, and we can see that there is nothing at this campsite other than ashes and blackened wood.

Half-heartedly Drygalski kicks at a charred branch. Fine flakes fly around our knees.

21 Picking up stuff off the ground. Branches. Stones. Stones that are a different shape to other stones and which you think for a moment might have some function other than being stones, when you examine their unexpected shape up close, when they are in your hand, when you've stood back up and the pain in your back from bending over all the time has subsided. And then you throw them away again and don't spare them a second thought. Here and there a plastic bag. Transparent sheaths for goods that are no longer available. Leaves.

22 Then Fürst breaks his ankle. There is no hole, no stone, nothing unpredictable, just a drainage channel cut across a country road, and the ditch is lined with metal, and the metal is not so rusty and covered in mud that you could have overlooked it. The snap is no different from the hundreds of snapping steps we took in the forest, but this time it is accompanied by an additional short cry and then panting, and then we see him trying to put pressure on his foot again, his face contorted with pain, and then we see how he shakes his head: no, he can't do it. He hops along on one leg for a short distance, as if there were a bench somewhere, or an easy chair or a bed. As if he had almost made it. Just a little farther and you can rest and we'll bandage your foot, and you can stay in bed for a while and rest up. And then he can't hop on one leg any longer. We're all weak and haven't eaten in

a long time. And he falls forward onto his hands and knees. He freezes for a moment, and we can't tell if his back is quivering because his ankle hurts or because he's sobbing, and then he slowly sinks down onto that thick, wet grass. First his belly, then his chest, then his face.

He lies there for a couple of minutes, completely still. Gruber goes over to him, bends down, but Fürst just shakes his head. He cries out once more, when Drygalski carefully tries to touch his foot, presumably in order to see how badly he is hurt, but his scream is so full of rage and finality that we all understand. His foot is twisted at an unnatural angle, to one side, and it's obvious that you can't walk on a foot like that. The only thing you can do with a foot like that is lie down. We stand. We stare. We don't say anything.

Before we move on, we drag him to an oak by the side of the road. We lean him up against the tree, facing the misty peaks of the Wilder Kaiser or the Hahnenkamm or whatever mountain range it is that is slowly emerging from the fog. We turn his head in the direction he was looking when he failed to notice the drainage channel that rendered his foot unusable, and later, once his features, which now are distorted in agony, have relaxed, he will see the very mountains that he saw when he was still in possession of two healthy legs and the only thing that was out of joint was the world. Then we leave. We leave him sitting in the wet grass, and we hope that the night won't be so cold that he will die in the dark. But cold enough that not long after sunrise it will be over.

23   I imagine Fürst, a few weeks ago, waking up before the alarm goes off. He gets up right away, stretches, brushes his teeth, showers, gets dressed. He puts on a clean pair of jeans, a clean shirt, a clean jumper. He blow-dries his hair and combs it. He applies some gel. His hair looks good. His clothes fit perfectly. Fürst is a good architect. I imagine him leaving his spacious, tastefully decorated flat. It's affordable because it's not central. Fürst is a man who is careful with money, but who will also buy himself something good from time to time, because he knows what's good. I imagine him getting into his Audi A4, which he bought second-hand, driving up the ramp of the underground garage and heading into town, and he is glad to have got an early start because today he's going to ring Dengler's doorbell before Dengler can call him, because Dengler's been calling him every day for the past week despite the

fact that it's been dry and no rain has been forecast, and despite the fact that both of them, Dengler and Fürst, have known for a week that Fürst would be coming to see Dengler on this Friday morning, bright and early, at 7.30, and after all they've both got other things to do. Dengler works for Siemens and really Fürst is already onto the next project. Dengler has bought himself a flat in a new housing development, which has been finished for ages, but during the last big storm his balcony got flooded, and that won't do. I imagine that Fürst doesn't have anything against Dengler, but he doesn't like it when people who don't know anything about certain things feel the need to dole out advice about those very things about which they know nothing, particularly when it comes to what looks good and what doesn't. Sure, tastes differ and you've got to respect that, but if people are so sure about how everything is supposed to look then why do they bother hiring an architect? With some people, you can't even imagine the ideas they have – they want to put a Doric column in the middle of the parking ramp, or an oriel on a flat roof. But a balcony that doesn't drain properly, that's obviously a problem. I imagine that in this case Fürst is happy to come and take a look. After all, Dengler paid for high-quality work and that is what he received. In terms of the planning in any case, that much is certain. And it's not like you can always keep an eye on everything those Hungarian foremen, the Polish supervisor and the Montenegrin cement mixers are doing. They just say, yes, yes, but have no idea what you're talking about. How many times has Fürst had to make them tear open freshly boarded walls because they simply don't give a damn that they're still supposed to put the cables in, or windows, or moulding. I imagine all the things that go through Fürst's head, at the wheel, on the thorough-fare, on a sunny morning on his way to work. And then the light turns amber, and Fürst begins to accelerate but then sees that he won't make it. The light turns red, and then he brakes. His phone rings. He brakes harder, presses the clutch. His phone keeps ringing. He brakes even harder, and then his phone slides off the passenger seat and onto the floor, and Fürst shouts, Dengler, you fucker! He overshoots the stop line by at least a metre. And then Fürst retrieves the phone and answers it, and says, Good morning, Herr Dengler.

24 We come across a VW Golf II that's not completely burnt out. We take out the floor mats. We rip off the number plates. We gather together the charred remains of the carpeting into a pile on the ground. We stomp on the bumper till it comes off. We use the number plates to cut the wiper blades off the metal arms. We read: Bosch. We put the rubber with the floor mats. We tug on the charred seat belt. The retractor dispenses six feet of intact belt strap. We pull it out as far as possible and then cut the strap, again with the number plates. We remove the headrests from the front seats. The cushion is completely incinerated. We wrench the metal rods apart. We use the rods to pry the seat belt's melted plastic catch out of the holder. We tug at the soot-covered wheels. We smash the windows.

Look, I say.

I'm holding the detached steering wheel. We all stare at it for a while. Then I throw it on the grass, behind the rubber floor mats and the pieces of wiper blade. Then we move on, taking nothing with us.

25 The next day brings heavy rain. Through the gloomy film of the falling water we see a gigantic pit by the side of the road, and jutting out of the pit are walls, isolated, disconnected, and growing out of the walls are bridges of steel pipes. A tarpaulin is flapping in the wind, so that sometimes the rain pelts down on it and sometimes not. A rushing sound that comes and goes. I think of the ocean. Steel rebar is jutting out of the tops of the walls. And looking down at this construction site I come to realise for the first time that it's no simple matter to establish criteria with which to determine whether something is in the process of being built or dismantled. When something is half-finished it is precisely only ever halfway to being finished, and however big or small the distance is to being something, it is the same as the distance to being nothing.

Let's go, says Golde.

26 Drygalski is holding a headless crow on a stick over a pile of burning leaves that is giving off far too much smoke, and says: Have you heard about these artists in Texas?

What?

In a small town called Marfa. They held assessment seminars with their richest and most loyal collectors to pick just seven who would get exclusive access to their new artworks.

No.

They're ultra-radical monists.

What?

They believe atoms are of greater value than people.

OK.

Which is why they will only give their new artworks to people who have signed a contract pledging to use them on themselves right away.

OK.

And only if they leave their entire fortunes to the artists.

OK.

The smoke is burning our eyes.

What kind of artworks are they? asks Golde.

Phallus-shaped cyanide capsules, says Drygalski.

Life-size? says Gruber.

What?

Never mind. For men or women?

For both. Radical monists are transsexual, of course.

Of course, I say.

The lukewarm, semi-putrid bird tastes lukewarm and semi-putrid.

Cyanide capsules, Gruber says after a while.

Yes? Drygalski replies.

How long does it take for something like that to work?

27 A couple of weeks ago we were playing our game. We had always played it when there were enough of us and we were in a cabin and had talked about everything there was to talk about at that moment. Golde got up to get a block of Post-its from his laptop bag. Fürst got some pens from the drawer in the kitchen cabinet. They put the Post-its and the pens in the middle of the table. Our hands reached for them, some faster, some more slowly. Some of us started scribbling right away, others thought long and hard. Some of us thought we had a particularly good idea, others didn't care how good the rest would think their idea was, or at least pretended not to. It was almost hot in the living room. The condensation in the air we breathed froze on the cold windowpanes. The glass showed distorted reflections of our backs and heads, of old, rustic utensils, pans over the stove, a cupboard full of elegant red wine

glasses. The Grubers had good taste.

On the Post-its we wrote names. The names of great women and men, of murderers, dictators and prophets. Names that every one of us knew, which we stuck to the forehead of whoever seemed most appropriate, or most inappropriate. The name of the game was: Who am I? And it always began with the same question: Am I still alive?

We sat and drank and laughed and asked the right and the wrong questions, with varying degrees of enthusiasm, and outwardly it was just like every other time, and yet something was different. We had lost some part of the unquestioned naturalness with which we used to sit, stand, walk and run together while the world came crashing in all around us and we would all see the same things, smell the same things, hear the same things. Back then we didn't even need to comment on what was happening. We knew each other and we knew exactly what we were thinking, what the others were thinking. We were here, and out there, in front of us, behind us, below us, were the others, the younger kids, the older kids, parents, girls, teachers, the black-board, the periodic table of the elements, homework, afternoons – short, colourful and loud in summer; in winter, empty and unending. Physical education, the patchy and uneven field, the running track, the dirty showers in the basement of the football club, the clods of turf in the studs of our football boots, the smell of the box for the jerseys, where, with feigned nonchalance in an unfamiliar changing room, we would look for our number before an away game; the disco at the youth club, the Turks, the Yugos, the unattainable girls who were probably allowing themselves to be kissed by the Turks and the Yugos long before we even knew how to hold hands; the cheap pizza delivery place by the pond in the shopping centre; the joy of being given the end piece of the leberkäse by the butcher across the street from school.

It was quieter than usual. The snow cannons over on the ski slopes weren't running.

28 We are sitting in the next cold storage locker, in the next supermarket, in the next village. We are thirsty because there is no water, we are full up thanks to a family-sized package of cold microwave fondue, and Drygalski says, It all comes down to the mind. All historical disasters can ultimately be traced back to mental illness. Neuroses, psychoses, hysteria. It starts with the witch trials and ends with the Third Reich. Or rather, as we can see, it doesn't ever end.

Hmm.

Statistics have shown that the use of antidepressants in the Western world over the past ten years has increased by five hundred per cent. Five hundred per cent! Can you imagine?

Golde nods, as if to say, yes, that's a lot. The others' faces are shrouded in darkness. But you can hear that they're all still awake.

The latest scourge of mankind is called chronic fatigue syndrome. It's all too much for everybody, too complicated, too pointless. Most people just want to be left alone to watch TV and sleep. But that's no way to organise a society.

I think that's the only way to organise a society, says Golde. If you're watching TV, you're not out committing any crimes.

I don't know, says Gruber. He's not in the mood for a debate.

It doesn't matter anyway, says Drygalski. At any rate, I'm convinced we've entered a phase of collective depression. After the last, brief manic phase that was the Nazi period, we now have collective depression.

Why now? And why depression?

Because we were doing so well. When we were doing badly, we went manic. Now that we're doing well, we're getting depressed. That's how it always goes. Our minds are always at odds with the external world. It's a defence mechanism. It's the most normal, most fundamental principle of existence. We're all just electrons. We all want what we don't have; become what we're not; plus, minus; black, white.

In that case we must all be about to become very, very happy.

Why? Are you unhappy?

Are you happy?

29

Just this last bend and then we'll take a break. Around the bend: an overturned tanker. Ribbons of rubber hang off the heavy steel rims, frozen in mid-air, though they look like they are still turning. The wheel nuts are black with soot. I wonder what happened here, how such a large vehicle could simply have keeled over on a straight stretch of road, and then I notice the logs a short distance away from the tanker, sticking out of the ground at an angle; they have been sharpened and rammed into holes in the tarmac hewn for that purpose. On the right-hand side, by the hard shoulder, I see more logs and rocks that have been used to prop up the sharpened logs that are sticking out of the ground. It must have happened at night, or perhaps during the day. Perhaps there had been more of these ramps. Perhaps they extended all the way across the road. Perhaps the tanker had been unable to swerve, the front wheel coming off the ground, tipping the whole thing over. I imagine it must have happened slowly, as if in slow motion. The front wheel lifts off the road, there is a jolt and a crunch as the cab skids out to the left of the trailer, and then for a brief moment there is silence. At the sight of the traction unit pitched to the left in mid-air, you don't even notice the sound of the engine. All you notice is that it's brown and that the paint is starting to peel and that in the background, by the side of the road, there is a thick, dark green conifer forest. And then suddenly there is a loud noise, a hard, deafening boom, out of nowhere, and the noise doesn't trail off, it begins to fray, segueing into a grinding, a screeching and twisting, a stretching and breaking, and through this tapestry of unhealthy sounds comes another loud noise, more muffled and booming, and a new, steady screeching, and the twisting and breaking is gone, there is only a screeching, lasting an astonishingly long time, before diminishing, and when it all comes to a standstill and finally dies away, the tanker is no longer a tanker, it is no longer the artificial, practical product of human intelligence, assembled by machines, but more like a mortally wounded animal. A coughing and wheezing and a long, final exhalation.

I imagine it won't have taken long before they were there, the people in tattered ski jackets and hiking boots, cautiously emerging from the trees. The tanker slid a little farther, but they had taken it down, that was the main thing. I imagine that they went about their work at a leisurely pace. They were not in any hurry.

I imagine that the driver in the cab was desperate to get away, but he probably also had a broken leg, and so he had to lie and wait, and he knew what was coming, later, when the silver tanks were empty, holding neither fuel nor alcohol nor milk nor melted snow, holding nothing but air, and then they sucked the last bit of diesel out of the reserve tank and poured it on the cab, which didn't really catch fire at first, but soon began to burn, emitting terrible amounts of smoke, thick and excessive – a stupid, senseless, ostentatious fire, in which the driver's broken body slowly disappeared. I imagine that he didn't even scream.

Come on.

Golde is standing next to me. Drygalski and Gruber have gone on ahead.

30 That evening, Golde is the first to enter the ramshackle fishing hut we come across by a circular pond, surrounded by tall reeds, and of course he's the only one to find some dry wood in there, a chair, surprisingly still intact, and of course he immediately smashes it to pieces while the rest of us tear the mouldy tar paper off the broken beams and bend bunches of reeds in half, lay the paper on top of them and then ourselves on top of that. It is wet, and the pond stinks, but this is the softest bedding we've had in a long time. We nestle up close to one another, as we always do these days. None of us wants to freeze to death, although we couldn't say why exactly. We don't know what we're waiting for or what we hope to find on our trek through a landscape that is nothing but a constant reminder of the fact that nothing is as it used to be. Luckily, we don't ask any questions any

more either, we just lie there in the pale glow of Golde's burning chair, and I feel Drygalski in front of me and Gruber behind me, and then I hear Gruber say: Love is a funny old thing.

It's your own expectations that are the problem, says Drygalski.

Nacho is too brutal for my taste, says Gruber. All that blunt violence is just his way of compensating for the length he's missing compared to Rocco. That silver bracelet. Those tattoos. His whole demeanour says: here's someone who's going to fuck you hard. And he does fuck them hard, but that's all. That's all that happens. He's too focused on that. On that one big question, that his excessive roughness and aggression seem to shout out again and again: Am I fucking you hard enough? Which is another way of saying: Does anyone love me?

I don't know, I say.

With Rocco it's something else entirely. He doesn't ask himself if he's fucking them hard. He doesn't even ask himself if he's fucking them at all. He grabs those women and the first thing he does is examine them very closely, nice and slowly. He examines them like rare, timid animals: butterflies, lanternfish, Komodo dragons. Like works of art. Like some new, totally alien life form. He feels, smells, tastes every inch of their bodies. Their badly shaved armpits, the soles of their dirty feet, their arseholes.

Nacho is interested in those as well, says Drygalski.

But he's only interested in their arses! And their vaginas, their mouths. To Nacho, everything else is irrelevant. Rocco wants to fuck their brains. Their DNA. It's plain to see that that man would die of sorrow if there were no more women. That's love.

I shake my head. But he fucks them harder than anyone else. He fucks them as if they were pieces of furniture. Who says you can't love furniture?

I sit up and look into the fire. You can no longer tell that the thing that is burning there was once a chair.

$3I$ The fear of being left behind, feverish and shivering, under a pile of damp leaves, when our legs can no longer carry us, when the path is forever uphill or our bodies' defences start to fail, is negligible compared to the effort that each individual step costs us. We hate the walking. We hate the ground that our feet must push out behind us and upon which we would have to stand if we were to stop moving. We hate the cool, clean air streaming into our lungs with each of our ever shallower and quicker intakes of breath, because it is the same air that makes us cold in the parts where we sweat. We hate the light that reveals to us just how much ground and forest and hill there is in front and behind and all around us, how much empty space above, how many of us are still here, how many are not, and how emaciated, dishevelled, ugly and stupid we look. All in all, we don't much care for this world any longer.

But still we continue diligently to take one step after another into it.

32 The morning after our arrival in the cabin one of us made breakfast while the four others watched. Don't let the oil get so hot. More bacon with those eggs. Less onion. More eggs. Less bacon.

We ate. Then we began to wait for our weekend to be over. We looked out over the valley. Somebody smoked a cigarette. We messed around in the snow for a bit. We looked out over the valley. We made a snow bar; for a while the task repositioned us completely anew here on the mountainside, in the Alps, in the universe. Once the bar was finished, we each hurriedly poured ourselves a wheat beer and stood around this white cuboid jutting out of the steep slope. The weather was so-so, but at least it wasn't snowing so you could stand to be outside. Golde, Fürst, Gruber and I drank our beers or looked at one another, our gazes jumping from face to glass to face, and whenever we weren't holding our glasses to our mouths, we would smile at one another. Drygalski stood for a long while staring silently over the valley, and then he said: What a view, eh?

33 I wake up. The cold and the damp of the ground feel familiar, as does the tarpaulin against my hand and my cheek, and my mouth has been much too dry for too long for any saliva to have dribbled out overnight. Just to stay like this for a while longer. Not because it's comfortable, but because getting up will have such terrifyingly little effect on my mood, my body temperature, my hunger.

And then suddenly everything changes once again, all the colours, sounds, smells, from one moment to the next, and the sky makes a noise and fine drops begin to fall, sideways, to the rhythm of the wind that has come up equally suddenly. It is raining. In our situation – wrapped in tattered tarpaulins beneath a leaky roof made of half-heartedly interlaced branches, waiting for a time when we're finally dry and warm or else dead

– this occurrence represents something of a disappoint-ment. But somehow it makes us happy to see how the world continues to do what it does completely without our assistance.

We eat whatever we find. We eat a dog that's been beaten to death. We eat two pigs that have been shot in the head. A half-burnt sheep. There is something degrading about eating things that just happen to be dead. Sure, a wiener schnitzel is dead too, but it was killed in order to be eaten. The animals that we consume, against our will, sometimes having to suppress our nausea, sometimes not, are just dead. Independently of us. They would have died one way or the other, regardless of whether we came along, picked them up, ate and digested them. Our ancestors were hunters, farmers, butchers. We are nothing but overgrown bacteria.

34 In the distance we see a pylon with several dark spots up at the level of the power lines. We get closer. We see the road leading away to the right, over the ridge, cutting what seems like an unnecessarily wide swathe through the trees on the mountainside. Above the road, eight power lines slice through the grey sky, leading away up the mountain to our left, where in a long, soft arc they disappear into the mist. We get closer. The dots on the pylon become clumps. Like drops of spilled electrical current. Two larger clumps where the cables meet the pylon; six or seven smaller ones farther down. The ground is also littered with bodies of all shapes and sizes. We see now that they are black. The ones hanging from the pylon too. We stop and look up. The clumps are clusters of burnt human bodies, fused together and with the cables and steel. Hard to tell how many. They're too burnt, contorted, shrivelled. Some of

the smaller clumps have sharp appendages sticking out of them, like the stumps of broken branches.

Feathers, says Drygalski, prodding a charred bird with his shoe.

Do you think there's still electricity in those wires, says Gruber.

There's one way to find out, says Golde, looking up.

We move on. That evening we sit shivering in a bus shelter. Rain drums on the roof. We huddle together, take the four tarpaulins off our four torsos and wrap them around the single communal body that we now are. Below, eight cold legs. I close my eyes. Just before falling asleep, I hear Gruber's voice: Probably the people got fried by the current first and then the birds came to eat their burnt bodies and that's when they got fried themselves.

Maybe, says Golde.

Or maybe it was the other way around.

35 I think there are just too many things, says Gruber the following morning, and Golde emits a noise that sounds like a bad orgasm.

I mean, all this stuff everywhere. Who is supposed to want it all? Everybody's already got something, haven't they? Most people have got something, at any rate. Hardly anyone has really got nothing.

There have always been a lot of things, I say.

But not this many, says Gruber.

Hard to say, says Drygalski, and Gruber says:

Fuck it. I'm talking about something much more basic than the things themselves. The really uncanny thing about it all is deeper, you know. When I'm standing there, in my warehouse, and the brown boxes full of men's underwear are stacked all the way up to the ceiling, twenty feet high, that's a lot of stuff, obviously, but it's not really the amount that frightens me. Really, it's something else. And then I think to myself: all these boxes have got to go somewhere, and all of these Y-fronts in all of these boxes come from somewhere. I mean, they're not from here, they're just passing through my warehouse. These Y-fronts come from a factory near Izmir, and the packaging comes from Belgrade, and the cardboard boxes that I'm packing them into, they're from a paper mill outside Bruges. It's all recycled, but still. All that stuff. And then the DPD lorry arrives and every screw, every floor mat, every fucking pebble under the brake pedal has travelled farther than an ordinary human being a hundred years ago ever went in his whole life. That's fucking insane, isn't it?

Well, I say.

It is, though, Gruber says. When everyone always wants to go somewhere other than where they are, and are always coming from somewhere other than where they want to go, then how is anyone ever supposed to know where they are?

Where's home, you mean?

No, I mean the movement as such, the constant back and forth, the never-being-able-to-stay-put-for-five-minutes. Let's assume the world is an organism and all of us and

all of our products are the molecules that make it up –
then the world would be running a high fever.

Drygalski shakes his head: Apart from us, nothing else
around here is moving very much.

I can see that. I don't mean now, obviously. I mean
before. I mean, we should have seen this coming. And
what would we have done then?

Later it begins to snow. Flakes of various sizes follow
various intersecting trajectories towards the ground,
blown, now gently, now not so gently, by the mercurial
wind. Twigs, branches and trees take up the movement
of the wind, and in the space between, in front of me,
I see three backs, with three heads lolling above them,
swaying through a gradually whitening forest, six
shoulders leaning alternately left and right, in direct
correlation to which of the feet below is touching the
ground. It doesn't look like a fever. More like an infi-
nitely slow falling. As if gravity no longer worked along
the shortest distance between a body and the centre
of the Earth but rather in gigantic, concentric circles
forever forcing us onward, farther and farther, around
the entire globe, and finally to our knees.

36 The last morning in the cabin had had something conciliatory about it. We thought we would soon be returning to our functions in society, we were looking forward to our own beds, with our own televisions or else our own bedtime reading. Some of us were also looking forward to seeing our wives. And so we packed with gusto and were relieved that we weren't all that hung over. There was a time when we would have had shots, not just beer. One of us would have puked. And the mountain air is pretty good for you, after all. We fastened the straps on our backpacks and placed them by the front door. We made the beds, we rolled up our sleeping bags, did the dishes in ice-cold water, and when our hands went numb one of the others would take over. We made one last pot of coffee, and poured it into five mugs. We washed up the pot right away, took the filter out of the coffee

maker, wiped off the countertop, put the radio back on top of the cupboard. We turned off the electricity, and the water. First you closed the main valve, then you let the remaining water run out of the pipes in the kitchen and in the bathroom. One of us swept the floor. One of us tied up the rubbish bags and put them next to our backpacks by the door. Then we stepped out on the terrace with our coffee mugs, to take in the view one more time, and to assure ourselves that we were really here, all of us together.

We stood there, sipping our coffee, looking down into the valley, not saying anything. We stood there looking down into the valley. Steam rose from our mugs. The shapeless clouds. The snow. Your hand holding the cup, the one in your pocket. In the early morning, when you just step outside for a moment with your cup of coffee, you don't need a hat. The snow cannons were still off. It had been a nice weekend. But it was also OK that it was over. Perhaps this would be the last snow bar we ever built. Things we had to do on Monday. The cold on our heads. Thick, black smoke over the village in the valley. It was on fire.

37 No idea if this was an engine fire or an aerial bomb, says Golde, stepping into a reddish-brown puddle in his hiking boots.

Why an aerial bomb? There are no aerial bombs any more. The only place you might find one is during an excavation.

In the puddle around Golde's foot there is a charred hair clip. Gruber shoves Golde out of that mess. Drygalski pretends to look at the trees by the edge of the road, as he always does whenever things aren't entirely harmonious, and I stoop to pick up that little piece of metal with the wavy edges.

Today we've got missiles. Surface-to-air missiles, surface-to-surface missiles, air-to-air missiles, air-to-surface missiles.

Cruise missiles, says Drygalski.

Exactly, says Gruber.

Shut up, says Golde.

Click-clack goes the clip in my hand. The others stop for a moment. They weren't expecting to hear this sound in the midst of a discussion among grown men about modern weaponry, and it takes their brains a surprisingly long time to associate this sound with the child's seat in the burnt-out Fiat Multipla. Intercontinental ballistic missiles, I say. Right now they would probably be your best bet.

38

That's my stick, says Golde, pointing to my hand. Drygalski's eyes go wide.

I found it, I say. Back there next to that tree with the big patch of lichen, it was lying on the needles with one end sticking up in the air because the other end was lying on a root. I picked it up. I'm holding it in my hand at this very moment. How can you possibly say that it's your stick?

Give it to me.

Get your own, I say, but without any emphasis in my voice, without any real conviction, more like when someone asks you how you are and you say fine. Gruber pricks up his ears. Slowly he turns his head towards me and Golde. There is a glint in his eye, his features remain oddly cold yet tense, he wants something, you can tell, he has an urge, a desire, but it has nothing to do with questions about the nature of ownership – or the ownership of nature. He gets up and walks towards us, towards Golde and me and Drygalski, who is still sitting down, and who, like me, has a dry, brittle stick in his hand. Gruber comes closer. He wants to see what is about to happen. I sense an alertness inside me, a directedness that doesn't care towards what, a waiting that can suddenly become movement, lunge, kick, punch or bite. I think of dogs by the dinner table when a piece of meat is proffered. Then something snaps, and I see Drygalski holding out half of his dry stick to Golde, and Golde looks at it, and then he takes the stick and throws it in a high arc over his shoulder and carries on staring at Drygalski, and Drygalski very quickly looks away, and Golde keeps staring at him, and then he erupts into laughter, and then Gruber starts to laugh as well, and then me, we're all laughing and Drygalski is scratching his chin and looking up at the tree he's sitting next to as if he were with the bark beetle commission. He's forcing his eyes to follow the grooves in the bark: aha, this one swerves to the right. And Golde is clutching his belly, and Gruber is slapping his knee, and I thump my fist on the soft forest floor, ha-ha, it's so soft, and I give it another thump, harder this time, and we laugh and laugh and wait for something to come and resolve itself the way it always used to when we laughed, but nothing is resolved. Then we stand there panting, like after a fight. Even though I'm exhausted, tonight I can't sleep. Tonight I keep my eye on Golde.

39 A supermarket with a broken glass door is a familiar sight by now. We know how to navigate them safely, and just because we're hungry that's no reason to rush. Admittedly, the hole in the glass is low down, you have to duck, really you have to do more than duck, you have to crawl, on your stomach, and Golde doesn't like to crawl. In any case he crawls very hastily and fitfully, or just awkwardly somehow, impatiently, and as soon as he thinks he's through he jumps to his feet, but in fact he's not through, and the long, sharp shard of broken glass in the door frame pierces his jacket, his jumper, his shirt. The shard pierces his skin, the muscles in his lower back, his kidney, and judging by the way he is screaming, probably some of the toxins that his kidney was filtering have seeped directly into some nerve ending or other. He lurches forward, he roars, falls, lies, twitches.

One by one we crawl through the hole that he has helpfully vacated, and Gruber, who is directly behind him, crouches down and lifts up his head and pulls the loud, twitching thing, which is what his upper body has become, into his lap. From the deep gash in his lower back downwards there appears to be no life left in Golde.

Drygalski and I come closer, slowly, uncertainly, filled with a sense of curiosity that I find a little unsettling. Golde's roars are growing louder and more high-pitched, until finally he is squealing, he is squealing so much that I look at him in disgust, lying there in Gruber's lap. I can feel my mouth contracting into the kind of expression you normally have just before you throw up. Luckily Golde can't see it, his face is buried in Gruber's crossed calves. He is trying to raise his head. He gives up and tries again and gives up again, and he tries it one last time and he gives up. And then he gives up. And he is screaming all the while, unbearably loudly, and I am startled, but then also relieved, when Gruber whispers to me, Give me the hammer. And just to make sure,

I say, What?, even though I heard him perfectly well the first time. Golde is screaming. Gruber says, Give me the hammer. Golde is screaming, and the others are standing around, and their body language says, We don't have all day, and Gruber yells, Give me the hammer, and then Golde yells as well, For fuck's sake give him the hammer, and then I pull the hammer out of my belt and give it to Gruber, and then the hammer comes down from a great height into Gruber's lap, and hair and blood spatter my face, and then it is quiet. I lick my lips. They are salty.

40 That night we can't fall asleep. And so we get up and keep going. It's slow going in the dark. We walk in single file. The one in front gingerly holds his arms out and follows the path, the others each place their hands on the shoulders of the one in front of them. After a while this strikes us as weird so we let go again. We let our arms swing by our sides and listen for the steps of the one in front of us. They sound soft, careful, uneven, they have no end and no beginning. Our feet drag across the soft forest floor. We don't even bother lifting them any more. We are stroking the surface of the planet. It's like we are trying to make up.

41 I imagine Golde, a few weeks ago, sipping a cup of coffee. The coffee tastes awful. Golde says: Good coffee.

The afternoon sun is shining through the blinds. The clients' clock strikes four.

I imagine Golde saying something to break the ice – Bang on time, for example – and I imagine the female client, let's call her Frau Huber, nodding and then looking at her husband, who gives Golde an expectant but not unfriendly look, wondering whether he means them or himself.

Do you still believe in retirement?

Ah, well, goes Frau Huber. Her husband goes, Hmm.

Golde laughs.

Father Christmas, God – sure, why not? But retirement? I'm afraid I'm going to have to disappoint you there. But of course you want to plan ahead. You're smart. That's why you're here today. That's why you called me.

You called us.

Right. But you told me: Herr Golde, please come on Thursday at four, and it is Thursday at four and here we are, having coffee, and we're going to see what we can do to provide some security for your retirement.

I imagine Golde leaning back in the armchair by the coffee table as if to show them what a secure retirement looks like. He takes another sip of coffee, and then his movements suddenly become very quick. He smooths his golden yellow tie, his hand pausing for a brief moment on his golden tie pin. He doesn't touch the matching cufflinks for now. Not until they sign, he says to himself. Then he bends down over the briefcase at his feet and pulls out two contracts.

Please take a moment to fill these in.

All right, says Frau Huber. Herr Huber looks sceptically over the top of his glasses. He begins to read. Then he says:

But.

Yes?

You haven't told us a thing yet.

That's true. That's because everything is clear. But I'll

be happy to tell you about it. I'll tell you everything you want to know. What would you like to know? That the population pyramid for Germany is currently more unstable than it would have been if the First and Second World Wars had occurred simultaneously? That the state pension funds have lost billions on their investments in emerging markets? That China has overtaken Germany as the world's largest exporter? That we will be facing deflation soon?

No, says Frau Huber. We know all that. We're not complete idiots, are we, Gerald?

I imagine her as speaking more loudly and confidently than before.

I was thinking of something more along the lines of a consultation, says Herr Huber. Different options. Just to know what they all are. That's also what the young lady who called us said: a non-binding personal consultation. That's what I would like. What is this thing that my wife has already half-filled in, anyway?

Herr Huber, Golde leans back, I appreciate your scepticism.

I'm not sceptical.

Yes, you are, and I thank you for it. I prefer working

with people who know exactly what they are doing. Who don't let anyone take them for a ride. People who won't just let you tell them how the world works. And they're the sort of people you want to make an effort for. I'm the same way. That's why I immediately felt at ease here.

A confiding glance at Frau Huber. She shifts her weight from one buttock to the other, smiles, or something to that effect.

Herr Huber. What your wife is filling in there is nothing other than what is going to preserve your standard of living in old age. It is the guarantee that you won't suddenly find yourselves empty-handed if and when the German state fails again. Wouldn't be the first time.

I imagine Golde laughing, and Huber not, and Golde thinking to himself, Tough nut to crack, but maybe he doesn't like references to the Third Reich, a Jew perhaps, or his grandma was killed in the bombing, or his grandpa killed in action. We'll see.

And of course I will explain the principle behind the investment type with the highest security and the highest yield for your retirement: Europe Central, the Rolls-Royce of central European property funds. Safe as houses. And I'll tell you about all the other things that are out there. But first I'd like to tell you what there won't be any longer, in five years: the euro.

Frau Huber laughs, Golde laughs with her. He's got her, but what about him?

So how does this fund work, exactly?

First of all, it's exclusively first-rate countries, first-rate locations, first-rate interiors. Germany, Scandinavia, Switzerland. None of that Mediterranean or Slavic rubbish.

Aha.

Guaranteed monthly returns from a predetermined age, in a predetermined amount, depending on the premiums. Alternatively, you can also receive a one-time lump sum. Who knows, perhaps you're dreaming of finally getting that Porsche for your retirement? Or a yacht? If you've worked hard all your life, you should be able to reward yourself later.

I'm on disability.

But you would work if you could!

And where exactly does my money go?

Your contributions will be invested in a fund. It's like a big cake that everyone bakes together, and then in the end everyone gets a piece.

And what are the ingredients?

As I said, it's nothing but first-class properties in exclusive locations: Hamburg-Ottensen, Berlin-Mitte, Zürich Goldcoast. The crème de la crème, you know what I mean? You won't see any of those urban waste-lands like Neuperlach or Hasenbergl.

I grew up in Hasenbergl.

And of course it used to be beautiful there. Until all those, well, how should I put it, in any case when they brought in all those foreign workers they didn't always think ahead, you know, Herr Huber. I mean, let's be honest, is that really still your Hasenbergl?

No, you're right about that.

Is this still your Germany?

No.

You see?

But you want me to invest in this Germany?

In the good parts.

Aha.

The risk is spread out across the most reliable and most sought-after real estate companies in the entire region of central Europe. Diversified, we call it. Nothing can go wrong. If they all go belly-up we'll have much bigger problems to worry about.

You mean if the next world war comes we won't even get a pension?

Oh, Gerald.

Herr Huber. If the Third World War comes, nobody anywhere will be getting anything. I assume that's clear. But I also think that we can expect our politicians to be more, well, maybe not sensible, but at least not entirely idiotic.

From your mouth to God's ear.

Gerald, I want to do this.

I don't.

Fine, then don't. I'm doing it.

Do what you want.

I imagine Herr Huber getting up and making for the door.

So you'll be sitting pretty if I die, but I'll be left with nothing.

I imagine Herr Huber stopping in his tracks, and Golde thinking: Oh bless you, Frau Huber. Suddenly she even seems vaguely attractive.

Give it here.

I imagine Herr Huber taking Golde's fountain pen, and Golde touching his golden cufflinks.

Please excuse him, he can be so stubborn sometimes.

That's men for you, says Golde.

I imagine them sharing a laugh then, Frau Huber and Golde. All except Herr Huber. He just wants it to be over.

Would you like some more coffee?

Thanks, I'd love some.

42 The meadow is wet. We're walking. The meadow is soft and elastic. We are walking slowly. The meadow is endless and on a mild slope, disappearing into the thick greyish white. Withered, sodden grass, burnt perhaps. No, just singed. A broad hill comes into view, the same colour as the background, not high, five or six feet perhaps, running diagonally from left to right, too even, too straight, too wide, somehow artificial, and as we get closer we see that it really is made of the same material as the ground. A railway embankment. We walk up it. Smooth, wetly glinting tracks, running in perfect parallel to the horizon in both directions. The contact line poles have been felled and are lying on the grass. Decommissioned timber machines. We stand around on the embankment, unsure how to proceed, but then we decide that when these tracks were still in use they must have led somewhere. We decide

to follow the embankment. At first we walk unnaturally fast, taking two sleepers at a time. Unnaturally long strides. We make good progress, but we also tire quickly. Little by little we adjust our stride, taking just one sleeper per step. These are unnaturally short steps, we are moving unnaturally slowly, and the concentration it requires to ensure that each step hits a sleeper is tiring, even if we are moving slowly. I wonder briefly where all the little stones in the track bed come from. I wonder who brought them here and who mined them somewhere else, and how many there are per square foot, on this stretch of track, on all the tracks in the world, and I begin to marvel at how many stones there are in the world and how many track beds and tracks and how many places they used to lead to, and then Gruber suddenly leaves the embankment, and the rest of us follow him, relieved. We don't need a destination. There wouldn't be anything there any more if we ever got there anyway. It's more important to be able to walk the way we want to walk, and so we keep walking across the thick, wet grass. We walk slowly and steadily.

43 We hear the rumble from a long way off. It is coming from a group of clean, new buildings surrounding an old Tyrolean farmyard. White walls, metal roofs. Stables, possibly. Of course we are afraid. We haven't heard any noise in so long that didn't come from us, or the weather, and this noise isn't particularly reassuring. A metallic rumble, steady but somehow off kilter. I can't say exactly what I think sounds wrong about it. It just seems to me that the noise isn't in harmony with itself, it doesn't sound the way it should, the way it was intended. It sounds forced, excessive perhaps, like a car engine in neutral doing three thousand revs at a stop light.

We approach with caution. The steel sliding doors on the first building are locked and we can't get them open. The windows are narrow barred slits ten feet off the ground. When we get to the second building we can hear that this is the source of the noise. We circle it once. The rumble stays equally loud and hyped up. In the rear we discover an unlocked wooden door. We enter. Suddenly it's very loud. The little side room in which we find ourselves smells powerfully of diesel. The rumble is different in here, deeper and richer, this sounds like an engine just doing its job, no more and no less, and when I see the diesel generator I think to myself, that's a bog-standard diesel generator, the type you see on farms throughout Europe being used for all sorts of perfectly ordinary tasks.

What's it running, Drygalski shouts over the noise.

A particle accelerator, Gruber shouts back.

What? Drygalski shouts.

A top-secret facility for producing black holes. A kind of unofficial emergency exit in case of a global catastrophe. The only way out of this shit. Finally, we've found it.

What? Drygalski shouts.

How the fuck would I know? Gruber shouts back.

The next door leads into the main space, and we are relieved because we've identified the rumble as the perfectly ordinary sound of a perfectly ordinary generator, doing its thing in a perfectly ordinary way, and in the central space we see a perfectly ordinary mammoth steel tank connected to perfectly ordinary tubes, each leading to one of the milking stations arranged in a large circle around the tank, at each of which there would ordinarily be a perfectly ordinary cow, but now they are all lying there, the cows, and they do not look ordinary, but it is still a perfectly ordinary milking machine that they simply forgot to switch off when the world ended, and it is still sucking and sucking, the way milking machines ordinarily do, despite the fact that there is nothing coming out of the cows, hasn't been for quite some time. Underneath their hides they are all empty except for their bones. Old, wrinkled cow costumes with slightly overlarge heads, long after Halloween. Orange slime is oozing out of the tank's overflow valve. It stinks.

44 On a narrow stone bridge we see a coach, wedged in between waist-high walls. Far below, a brook babbles romantically. We laugh. The vehicle's gigantic front end, the potholed road before it, on either side the old stone walls.

What an idiot, says Gruber.

We don't dare to try and squeeze past the coach across the twenty-centimetre-wide wall above the twenty-metre drop. So we smash the windscreen with a piece of the rock jutting out of the slope at the side of the road, between the tarmac and the trees, where year after year the soil is loosened and washed away by the snowmelt.

We wrench the blanket of splintered safety glass out of

its frame. We step on the bumper. Tentatively, we reach into the empty rectangle above the radiator grille. Our hands grip the dashboard. Carefully, we pull ourselves up and into the coach. On the floor there are chocolate wrappers and empty bags of crisps and a couple of empty water bottles. In row three we find a light brown scarf. Drygalski stuffs it into his bag. Gruber finds a suede glove in the luggage rack. Just for fun I turn the key in the ignition. With a start, I duck for cover from the loud music – *heeeeeeeeey hey baby (uhh, ahh)*. I quickly turn it back off.

If we hadn't smashed the windscreen, this would have made a good shelter for the night. Now the wind is whistling in through the open front and out through the open side door in the back. The coach happened to come to a standstill at a point where you could just about open the door and get out one by one. The luggage compartments, by contrast, are inaccessible, wedged in between the dented metal of the chassis and the stone wall of the bridge. We get out. We stop at the rear for a moment. The engine cover is open. We stand for a while and examine the engine. It looks exactly how I would have imagined the engine of a tourist coach to look. We close the cover. There is something reassuring about the sound.

The narrow road winds its way down the mountain in steep serpentine coils. Farther down it widens out. The valley opens up before us. We can see the first passenger. He is lying in the middle of the road as if placed there for our benefit. His head resting on his rucksack, his arms crossed over his chest. His clothes and face are covered in a thin layer of snow.

The valley gets wider. We are nearing a village. We see more and more people. It seems to me that there are too many to have all fitted into a single coach. But I may be wrong. I don't count them, and I also have no idea how many people you can fit on a coach.

They are lying on the road, all in a row, as if the one in front had stopped and the rest had lacked the courage to go past him, or the strength, and so they stayed there, in the lee he provided, until he was too cold to stay standing and then they huddled behind the second, the third, the fourth, until at some point the fifth also lay down, on the four others in front of him, slowly, as if on a well-made bed.

They are sitting in the ditch by the side of the road, leaning against the slope. From the road all you see are brightly coloured hats, but from the curvature you can tell that there are still heads underneath them, frozen solid in their dreams. Two are lying on the tarmac, one on top of the other at a right angle, as if at the last moment they had wanted to pray, and for want of a cross had decided to make one out of their own bodies. They are sitting by the side of the road, leaning against the walls of the houses, one resting his head on the other's shoulder, as if they were simply asleep, peaceful and soft, and white. They are lying in front of closed doors, in open doorways, on doormats and thresholds, on the narrow pavements once filled with passers-by. Under the empty, smashed window of the butcher's shop. They are leaning against the wall of the village cemetery, they are lying behind it, in rotting wooden coffins beneath heavy tombstones etched with numbers that soon no one will know the significance of. They are lying in the fields around the village, down in the valley, in the wooded slopes, on the cliffs above. Since time immemorial they have grown, withered and decomposed here in this region, blown by the wind all over the country, and the neighbouring countries, the whole planet. They are in the trees. In the grass. In the snow. In the rain that is beginning to fall on the snow.

45 We are standing side by side at the edge of the road, urinating into the bushes.

When this is all over I'm going to design women's urinals for restaurants and get filthy rich, says Gruber.

I say: Don't they already have those?

No idea. All I know is that there's always a queue for the ladies' whenever I go past one. At the cinema, after the movie, for example.

I once saw a woman pissing in the men's urinal, says Drygalski. She just went and stood facing away from the urinal, leant forward a bit and lifted up her skirt.

And what did the men do?

They just carried on pissing.

We carry on pissing.

Drygalski says: When this is all over, I'm going to make a TV show. It'll be set up like a contest, but really it'll be a sociological experiment.

What?

The question I'm interested in is: How important is a person's address to them? Their postal address. Is it more important for most people to live in a nice house or to live on a street with a nice name?

What?

We'll give away houses. Brand-new, nice houses. Just like that. All in a housing estate with the shittiest street names imaginable. Imbecile Drive, Arsehole Avenue, Paedophile Crescent. We'll have to build the estate specially for the show.

And then?

And then there'll be two contestants. The houses get better and better, the street names worse and worse. The first one to hit the buzzer on their podium gets a house.

And the other contestant?

Gets a different house.

And where's the contest in that?

You've got to be quick on the buzzer, otherwise you'll get the crappier name.

But the nicer house.

Exactly. The point is to establish the ratio between the

need for luxury and the need for social prestige. Presumably everyone will have a different pain threshold. It would be interesting to watch.

What a load of rubbish.

No, I'm serious. If someone were to give you a flat at Haemorrhoid Street 2a, would you accept it?

Absolutely. And then sell it.

And who would want to buy it?

Some Chinese pension fund. Golde always says they'll buy anything. Used to say.

Hmm. Maybe.

Beside me, Gruber makes measured shaking movements, leans forward, buckles his belt and stands up straight.

Maybe that's the only good thing about our situation.

What is?

There won't be another real estate bubble for decades.

46 A village on fire is really not such a complex phenomenon. Villages are composed of houses. Houses are composed, in part, of flammable materials. They contain wood, textiles, polyethylene, cotton, particle board, paper, leather, rubber, hemp, alcohol, protein, keratin, hair. And bones, sometimes. There were times when burning villages were a regular occurrence. Burning cities, too. But here and now what we were seeing in the valley below was so completely out of context for our usual perceptual experience that we were incapable of any reaction. Perhaps the sight of a single burning house would have been easier to comprehend, would have more quickly allowed us to make use of our faculty of speech, of our hands and feet. I'm pretty certain. A solitary house on fire would have been something else entirely. Two houses on fire? Sure, why not, so long as they were right next to each other.

But there were more than two houses on fire here. The entire village was on fire, in its entirety, as it lay there, in the valley, by the railway line, eight hundred metres long by three hundred metres wide, fifty to eighty houses, former farmhouses, inns, offices, the post office, the train station, winter sports outfitters, florists', holiday flats for the detested Dutch and German tourists. There seemed to be a plume of smoke rising from every single roof, all merging just above the village to form a gigantic cloud that gyrated around several crooked axes and was so thick that it seemed almost solid.

Drygalski lit a cigarette. Must you? asked Golde, and I wasn't sure whether he was bothered by the smoke – after all, we were out in the open – or whether he simply found it tactless in the face of the thick plumes of smoke in the valley below which were growing by the second and which were now beginning to bring home to us what it means for every house in an entire village to be on fire: people were dying.

Once we were able to move again, we quickly poured out the cold coffee. We just poured it out over the railing, into the snow, and I could see that the stains were brown, but to me they looked like blood. Then we went inside and wiped the mugs clean with Drygalski's paper tissues, put them back in the cupboard. Something was making us hurry, some unspoken, illogical urge, since why would we want to leave here in a hurry to go down there, when down there everything was on fire and not here? Golde stayed outside and looked at the village, which was burning away steadily, the smoke growing thicker and more amorphous and harder to ignore. Drygalski went and stood beside Golde. Golde said, Have you got one of those for me? Me too, me too, me too. Now we were all smoking. It was almost as unbelievable as what we were witnessing down in the valley, but somehow it also made sense. After all, right now what we had to do was stay put, watch and think. Wait until we were capable of deciding what to do. It's nice to have something to do during such moments. Gruber and Fürst were coughing.

Let's go down to the car, then we'll see.
OK.

Fog was descending on the trees, down from the clouds above the peaks. We first saw it on the cliff face above us, and as we began our descent it enveloped us. We moved slowly. Walking downhill is bad for the knees. And for morale. Whereas each step up the mountain represents a small victory over gravity, going down is a long series of defeats against solitude, the need for comfort, your work calendar. We walked in single file. Our pace was significantly slower than it had been three days earlier on the way up. The one in front was not in front because he wanted to lead the others, because he wanted to be the first, but because everyone else wanted to be behind him. The one in front was slowing down, steadily, secretly, in the hope that someone would overtake him, and because he didn't want anyone to notice. The others slowed down too.

We were walking down into the valley. The snow was melting. Every once in a while we would stop and listen to noises that were telling us, Don't go down there, go back up, far up, hide. Gunshots, screams, looting, rape, murder. Then in our heads we would laugh at our over-active imaginations and carry on down into the valley through the slushy snow. A village was on fire. That was all. It could have been a series of unfortunate events. Two rival pyromaniacs, each setting fire to the other's house at opposite ends of the village in the middle of the night, and then an unfavourable, erratic wind. It could have been a collapsed overhead railway wire, a high-voltage power line, telephone lines, ISDN, fibre optic cable, something with something else flowing through it, nodes, an explosion at a distribution substation, flames darting out of every wall socket in every house. It could have been an incendiary bomb dropped inadvertently by an American jet fighter from the Rammstein airbase, the pilot having lost his bearings over the snow-covered landscape. It could have been a troupe of marauding Tyrolean boy scouts, thirsty for the blood of Dutch and German winter tourists – Why don't you come as often as you used to? It's your fault we're going broke. Take that. Die.

The absurdity of your own fears is the greatest comfort. Painting a mental image of all the things that will never come to pass is the best means of ensuring that they never come to pass. The last turn before the mountain road. Remind me exactly why I believed that, again?

The car: ashes and metal.

Without a word we turned around. Without a word we went back to the cabin. Without a word we locked and bolted the door and closed the curtains. As we sat in a semicircle around the stove, Fürst was the only one brave enough to admit that he was scared by being the first to say what we were all thinking: And what are we going to do now?

We'll go over the ridge, said Golde.

What is there on the other side?

Maybe a village that hasn't burnt to the ground.

47 Leaving the forest behind we come into a wide valley. The mountains on either side disappear into the low clouds, in front of the mountains lies a foggy forest, in front of the forest, foggy fields, on the fields, ugly industrial buildings in black or green or grey. The windows are mostly broken, here and there signs of a fire. Through the middle of the valley runs a road. On the road: cars. Empty, stationary cars, as far as the eye can see. They are all facing in the direction of the valley mouth. Three columns across both lanes. No one seems to have been expecting any oncoming traffic. They stand there unmoving, silent, from left to right. We stop and look at the scene for a while. Then we fall in.

We move past this abandoned outbound traffic jam. The road is slightly elevated and perfectly straight. The view would be nice if it weren't so foggy. To our left there is a field, a barbed wire fence and the corrugated iron façade of a factory building. To our right, the stream, then the field, the forest. Behind us, the road and the cars. Ahead, more road and more cars. In the distance, at the head of this endless line of stationary vehicles, something emerges from the fog: something compact, thick, chaotic. A big pile. Or a small mountain. We draw nearer. A multicoloured mountain. We draw nearer still. A multicoloured mountain of metal. We draw even nearer.

The line of cars beside which we are walking leads to a knot of cars that have come to a standstill next to, in and on top of each other. Crushed cars, overturned cars, cars that have been pressed together, wedged together, bumpers tangled in wheel wells, bumpers tangled in engine bonnets, in dented driver's side doors, in severely dented passenger side doors, bumpers in bumpers in twisted boot lids upon torn-off car doors and on top of that rusty undercarriages, exhaust systems, wheels thrusting skyward and cracks, fissures and rifts in the crimson red, racing green, pearl white or obsidian black or in cheaper colours without trademarked names, dirty wounds that reveal that even the most dynamic SUV is really nothing more than a hunk of metal driven by fire. Pieces of broken safety glass everywhere, astonishingly evenly distributed, like sharp, bright-sounding snow.

The mind's childish hope that staring for longer will offer answers. We move closer.

It looks like more and more cars had forced their way onto the roundabout. It looks like the drivers in the cars that were already on the roundabout were no longer willing, or able, to leave. At any rate they wouldn't let any more cars in, and there were more and more cars that wanted to get onto the roundabout, from all four directions, and every once in a while one would manage to squeeze in, and they started going faster and faster around the roundabout, wondering as they passed each of the four exits whether it wouldn't be possible to break out, but from all four directions there were hundreds of other cars, thousands, stretching from each of the four exits to the horizon, waiting, as cars do, in the unmoving traffic, fathers determined to keep their nerve, mothers determined to trust their husbands to keep their nerve, children acutely aware of their parents' nervous tension and equally aware that this tension was unlike any other they had ever experienced, and who were therefore determined to believe the lies their parents told them: I'm sure we'll be moving soon.

They must have waited a long time. They must have waited until their fear was so great, their enforced inactivity so intolerable, and their rage at the ones who had made it onto the roundabout so strong that they could no longer care about anything. They must have waited until they realised that nothing mattered anyway, either because they were still able to think rationally and understood that the reason no one was exiting the roundabout was that no one knew where to go, because there was another car coming from every direction, lots of other cars, or else because they just couldn't go on, because they had been accelerating and braking for so long now, accelerating and braking, accelerating and braking; because they had crept along inch by inch, always keeping their eye on the roundabout that must lead somewhere, they had been accelerating and braking, and when they had almost reached the roundabout they could see that the roads coming from the right and the left were packed with cars but they couldn't see what the road on the far side of the roundabout looked like, the road leading straight ahead, and who knew, maybe that one was open, it was always possible; from each of the four roads leading onto the roundabout there was always one exit that was hidden from view, and, after all, there were always cars going round the roundabout; wouldn't they be at a standstill if there were really nowhere to go? And now the people ahead of them are moving again, and so now they are moving too, and now they just have to get out of here, to somewhere else, anywhere where things are different, no matter where, no matter who else is there, we'll figure something out, we just have to get out of here as fast as possible, there's no future for us here, we know that, back there it's all over. And then they all accelerated at once.

Where did all the people go? Drygalski asks.

48 That evening we are sitting in the soft sand of a practice bunker on a golf course. We dig a small pit. We reach into the plastic bags hanging from our belts for little shreds of paper and thin birch twigs, and from our coat pockets we produce pieces of MDF shelving, thinly chopped wood salvaged from Scandinavian stoves in holiday rental flats, and the folded lid of a box of Trivial Pursuit Genius Edition. We place everything carefully in the pit, in the shape of a pyramid, first the paper, then the cardboard, then the twigs, then the MDF, then the wood. Gruber strikes a match and holds it to the shreds of paper. They catch quickly, the cardboard turning black until a blue glow begins to shine through before erupting in a tongue of yellow flame. Gruber blows gently on the pile, and small flames begin to form along the twigs, like Christmas tree lights on a necklace, the plywood burns quickly too,

the wood more slowly. When we see that everything is in order, we lean back, rubbing our backs against the sand which will soon no longer be as cold.

Drygalski says: It would be nice to get some answers, some time.

That depends, I say.

What do you mean?

Not all answers are answers.

What do you mean?

Well, there's this thought experiment. Imagine that an alien comes to Earth in the spring, just as the wildfires are raging in California. Towns are evacuated, helicopters fly back and forth with loads of water, lives are extinguished, people stand with their pets in their arms watching as their life's work goes up in flames, their eyes full of tears and their lungs full of smoke. The fire brigade is out in force. Men are killed fighting the flames. Medals are awarded. Someone is caught smoking in the forest and summarily lynched. The governor in an olive green jacket gives a rousing speech. Experts on CNN expound computer models of wind, drought and climate change, and on Fox News just wind and drought. But nobody can really explain why these fires keep recurring.

And the alien?

He says: Excuse me, but it's really quite simple. Of course there's always a fire. Your atmosphere is full of oxygen.

49 The valley was on fire. So we went up into the mountains. It was hard to keep going on an empty stomach, and we had no water, that would have been too heavy. We drank melted snow. In primary school we had learnt that that was bad for you, but we couldn't remember exactly why. Presumably because back then there was still acid rain and leaded petrol. Now there was no other option. It took three hours till we could see the ridge. One more till we reached the top. We stood on the arête. The snow was a fine powder up here, the wind was howling with discouraging brutality, and instead of the hoped-for reward of a panorama of pristine, unravaged countryside, we saw nothing but another valley full of low-hanging clouds. We began our descent right away, by default, since we were too tired to stand around up here, but carefully, because it was steep and the wind hurt our eyes and ears even though

we were wearing hats. The wind hurt our hearts as well, and our lungs. They were on fire. We kept going, we stumbled, we fell, we got back on our feet. We were up to our waists in the fresh snow here on the north face of the mountain. We would not have lasted long. One of us pointed to the towers of the ski lift, farther down, it must have an end point somewhere, and then we caught sight of the mountain station about a third of a mile farther down. The lift was out of service even though the snow was good, but having seen the village on fire we were not surprised to find the station completely deserted. After a moment's hesitation, Golde picked up a block of ice from the mound of cleared snow and smashed one of the windows in the door. We squeezed through the opening, watching out for the shards of broken glass. Golde never used to be in so much of a hurry. We were happy to feel the faint trace of warmth inside the station, and then we were annoyed that we had made such a big hole. Gruber rolled up the carpet by the entrance and with Golde's help used it to stuff the hole; an ugly, makeshift solution which served only to make us even more acutely aware of how unprepared we were for our new circumstances. The wind whistled past the black plastic sausage and around our legs. A wide staircase led down into a restaurant area with a panoramic view. Thick rubber mats padded each step, which seemed excessive without ski boots on. It was as if it had been designed for people with a tendency to fall down stairs, but at the same time we were glad because it was an indication that people had given thought to other people here as they built the staircase. One by one we passed through the turnstile into the abandoned canteen. Instinctively, we each took a tray from the stack. There was still beer, some old sandwiches and pickled cucumber salad. The cucumber slices were so soft you could practically drink them. We didn't mind; we were thirsty. The fat in the deep fryer was cold, but still looked inviting. We resisted the temptation. We sat down at a table by the window. The fog was so close that the glass looked soft. The food did us good. We could feel the nourishment descending into our stomachs, we could feel the warmth spreading there, even though we'd only had cold food. We could feel that our bodies now had some materials to work with, something to burn. And then we put down our forks and slurped the cucumber and the dressing straight out of the white porcelain bowls.

Now let's look for the boiler, said Drygalski, breaking the lengthening silence. The rest of us nodded hopefully, politely wiping our mouths – the last remnant of the illusion of dinnertime – with our hands, not our sleeves. We got up and walked, sauntered almost, through the restaurant. We were in good spirits as we ascended the ski-boot-proof staircase. We paused by the entrance; hadn't we seen some doors here when we came in? Yes, indeed: there they were, two of them. Somewhat larger than ordinary. Painted white. Probably just pressboard. That's good; wood can be broken. Golde leant against one of them, Gruber against the other. They each pushed off and fell back against the door, repeatedly, each time farther, falling back harder. When their shoulders began to hurt, they tried with their feet. Fürst and I went back to the restaurant and looked in the kitchen. It wasn't particularly clean. There were half-empty pots here and there, some pasta, a basket full of rock-hard pretzels. The gas had been turned off. No electricity either, obviously. By now we could hear the sound of Golde and Gruber kicking at the door all the way down here. With a dull feeling in our stomachs, Fürst and I went back up the too-soft stairs. Just as we arrived at the top, the right-hand door gave way, and suddenly we were a horde of raiders, ready for anything. Panting and blind, we stumbled through dark hallways and down stairs, until we arrived at another set of locked doors. Steel this time. Nothing to be done. Nope, nothing at all. Our offensive crumbled at the first real obstacle. And what a stupid obstacle it was. We hammered on the door, shouting and cursing. Fürst started crying. As we headed back, beaten and exhausted, I felt strangely relieved at the thought that we hadn't found the boiler room. It would have been much more dispiriting to find ourselves face to face with the five-hundred-thousand-euro high-capacity HVAC system in a modern Alpine ski hut, freezing cold, in our thirties, with advanced degrees in architecture and microbiology and absolutely no clue how to get the thing working.

The other wooden door led into the owners' apartment. Apart from a few pieces of traditional furniture and a television, it was empty. There were no clothes or blankets. They had even taken the mattresses. Not that we had expected to find a working Primus or a pack of firelighters, but perhaps some pieces of firewood or at least some newspaper. The only thing we found was a package of paper napkins decorated with blue and white diamonds, which we put on the stone floor in the kitchen and, holding a wooden spoon over them, lit first one napkin, then two, then three, then four at a time, each time bringing a moment's delight as the flame from the lighter caught the paper, quickly spreading but also growing less bright, and we smelt the smoke and watched the Bavarian colours slowly vanish, curling feebly out of existence without having been of any use to us. The spoon didn't even turn black.

Then the package was empty and the lighter astonishingly hot, and although we presumed it would be pointless, we waited for it to cool down and then held it up to the varnished chairs and benches and tables until it once again grew too hot, at which point we would again wait and try again and wait and try again, and of course it had no effect, even though the things were made of wood, for fuck's sake, but of course this wood had been approved for use in the catering industry by the local fire safety authority, a long time ago.

So we went back to the last place where we had felt good. Our table at the panorama restaurant. We cleared it, Fürst even wiped it. And then we waited.

Before the sun went down the weather cleared. It got colder. It got dark. Then it got cold. It got cold in a way that is hard to describe. When you have grown up in a Western country, you assume that you have sufficient personal experience to allow you to make appropriate use of the concepts 'cold' or 'freezing'. You're wrong. What we experienced that first night in the abandoned mountain station was something completely new to all of us. The empty dining hall. The white moonlit slopes outside the panorama window. How beautiful they were. And how we hated them and their beauty, because we could suddenly feel nothing but a visceral fear of death. And so we danced. The five of us. We danced. We danced in the darkened dining hall, we couldn't see each other's faces, we could hear each other's surprised snuffling, panting, in between panicked exhalations and careful inhalations, fresh air, cold, much too cold. And above all the disbelief that such temperatures were possible in an enclosed space.

We stayed on our feet all night, shifting from one numb foot to the other. We rubbed against each other, and our tiredness was infinite and not worth mentioning, it went without saying, a meaningless constant like gravity, of which it was the direct, definitive continuation, straight through into the middle of our consciousness: whoever falls down now won't be getting up. We stayed on our feet. When it got lighter, it got easier. The temperature didn't change at first, but clearly it is comforting to be able to see where you are when you die.

In the end we didn't die. For a while we stood still in front of the panorama window and saw that day truly was dawning. Then we went on our way. Our first footsteps in the snow sounded unreal. Breaking the thin frozen crust, the powder beneath compressing, the soft, slowly dissipating scratch of the miniature avalanches spreading across the gleaming slope. With every step it started anew, with every foot laboriously lifted out of the whiteness, times two, times five. A susurration. It was calm. We avoided making eye contact, fearing a confirmation of our own feelings. Now there was no greater comfort than the sight of a familiar back in front of you, leading away from this situation, slowly, stooped and uncertain, but still moving. We followed the support towers of the ski lift down the mountain. Under the large bullwheels we rested and listened for the sound that belongs to this place, but steel cables don't sing when they are standing still.

50 Walking through the snow on the slope. Breathing in. Walking on the slope through the snow. Breathing out. Walking on the slope, breathing in, walking through the snow, breathing out. Walk, breathe in, walk, breathe out, breathe in. Think about how slipping would be bad, breathe out. Slip, fall, breathe in, breathe out. Think about how bad it is to slip, breathe in. Freeze, breathe out, breathe in, breathe out. Snow in every minuscule crevice in your clothes and in your shoes, breathe in. Snow down the back of your neck, snow on your wrists, snow in your ears and mouth, breathe out. Think, You'll never be able to get back up, breathe in. Get up. Breathe out, breathe in.

51 We are finding it increasingly hard to put the characteristics of our bodies that distinguish us from one another into words. Concepts like character or personality no longer have any meaning in our little group. Conversations mostly revolve around establishing daily necessities: who'll get water, who'll make a fire, who'll find a dead animal for us to eat? The answers to these questions are 'me', 'you' or 'him', rarely anything so romantic as a proper name. Other questions become rarer. We have become a single will distributed among several bodies, and beyond the portion of that will that each of us carries there is no room in our minds for anything else.

The will to live.

52

When it is dark, we try to walk quietly. We don't know why exactly. We have never encountered anyone either by day or at night who might have heard our footsteps or been a threat to us, and by day we always just walk the way we walk. Because we can see that there isn't anything. At night we can't see anything, but that doesn't mean that there is nothing there. And so we move through the blackness, arms stretched out in front of us, trying not to step in places where there are twigs and branches that might crack. We have no idea where those places are.

Presumably the only thing keeping us together in single file now is our shared familiarity with the words that we have used with similar frequency and in similar ways for decades. Mum, dad, God, Hitler, *De Bello Gallico*, the second binomial formula, foreign trade balance and the citric acid cycle, depending on what we studied – it wasn't really until uni that we began to drift away from one another, each of us pursuing the path that we assumed would lead to happiness, or money. We were always confident we would be able to turn around at any time, just let go, and then we would be back to what there was before there was what there is: us.

Us, so fearless.

Us, so full of laughter.

Us, with the coolest trainers in the whole school.

Us in the car cruising down Hansastraße: how much for a blowjob, and what if these four boys want to watch? Fuck off.

Us, confused: when did it start being alcoholism, when did it stop being just partying? All those times we stayed up all night, all those buckets of vodka Red Bull, the Weißwurst breakfasts where each of us had only one sausage but four beers.

Us, so clever, so stylish, so elegant, taking our parents' season tickets to hear Smetana or Mussorgsky. So inventive, with our stag nights full of love and lots of feeling, surprises, abductions, costumes, parachuting and of course a stripper at the club at night.

Us men.

Us boys.

Us children.

Us, on our way home from school, on a Friday, talking enthusiastically about the eyes and hair and clothes of the girls in our class, about lines from rap songs, about football players, about cars we would never be able to afford, about parental subsidies for driving lessons, about how it was Friday, about the party we would be going to, later, see you at eight.

Us, on the bike path through the fields at sunset, somewhere between the beer garden and the youth centre. Us, pedalling ever faster. Us, one by one, breaking into the darkness of the forest, with nothing but the wind in our wide-open eyes.

Us, guided safely by our cries.

53

In a clearing, red, yellow and blue shipping containers are strewn across the forest floor, rust creeping up the sides from below. They are locked. My heart begins to race. This could be something decisive. These things, in this place, what's inside them; us, aimless, hungry and cold, in a situation we cannot properly describe because we don't know enough about it, and probably never will. Which is bad, very bad. But this here could be something good, something that could save us. Something warm, soft. Something beautiful. Of course it could also be disappointing. Something unsettling, or horrible. Something terrible, or else completely insignificant. Either way: it could be something.

Why haven't they already been opened? Gruber asks, before he spots the padlocks, and I wish I still had the hammer. More than I wish we still had Golde.

We need a rock.

So we look. For a rock. In the middle of the forest. In the forest you can find wood, fir needles, the occasional abandoned fridge, but not usually rocks. Not a rock big enough to smash a padlock.

Give it here.

Gruber inspects the stone I've found under a root. It's about an inch across. He holds it with the tips of his fingers and knocks it on the padlock on the first container – Hamburg Süd – pats it more like, tock-tock. It sounds like he's using the brass knocker on an old villa in Blankenese. He stops. He makes a fist around the stone, holding it so that a piece of it sticks out between his index and middle finger. A tiny piece of stone, a hint of the universal symbol of hardness. He strikes the lock carefully, meaning that he doesn't really strike it, he tries to move his fist with the stone towards the lock in such a way that the stone makes contact with it but his flesh does not. On his first attempt, he succeeds. On his second as well. On the third, which is harder, the first real strike, we do not hear the sound of stone on steel, but rather just a dull thud. Gruber cries out and jumps away, rubbing his hand.

From the forest comes the sound of something being dragged. Panting, a groan, the sound of branches being stepped on till they break, the small ones right away, the thicker ones only after a while. Then more panting, dragging, splashing and the reverberation of metal.

Give me a hand with this.

Drygalski drags a fridge out into the clearing. We bend over, our backs creaking, this isn't the way to lift something, then our knees creak too, and the dirty white shimmering block of metal glides towards the middle of the clearing, towards the container, towards the padlock.

The noise is impressive. The impact reverberates for a long time inside the container, and it seems unfair that the noise we have made should already be where we want to be but can't. Not yet. Another blow. Another blow. And another. The fridge falls on the grass with a dull thud. We pick it back up and smash it against the lock, actually hitting it this time for a change, the next two times we don't, and then we drop the fridge again and we leap to one side, getting our tired legs out of harm's way. Our knees creak. We pick it back up, bang it against the container again, and this time the lock breaks. We don't really dare to open the door. Golde is dead. Fürst got left behind. And Gruber and Drygalski aren't sure, so I raise the latch and carefully pull on the door. It swings open surprisingly easily. In the dim light we see something white, lots of white, boxes, blocks of white, faintly gleaming, metallic, with rounded edges. Refrigerators. A whole container's worth.

Later, a fire. There has to be a fire, there always has to be a fire when you have nothing to do besides carrying on exactly as before. The light in which civilisations are built and torn down. Really we ought to be dancing, but, as is so often the case, the euphoria is just in the mind. Just a word.

It wasn't easy getting the fire started, but the warnings printed on the packaging gave us hope and determination, and in the end it worked with the coolant from the compressors. In silence we wait for an explosion, probably because that's what happens on television. We have to keep moving because of smoke from the polyurethane insulation and the vinyl chloride lining gets in our noses. There is no explosion. When it gets dark, we can see the glow of the fire inside the open container on the surrounding trees, a reddish-yellow quivering square at the edge of the clearing, like a door to a better, warmer forest.

At dawn Drygalski shakes me by the shoulder and then Gruber, and then we get up. Come with me, he says, and we go right up to the container, which now has just a trickle of smoke coming out of it, and then he goes and stands with his back against the side of the container and folds his hands to give Gruber a leg up, and then me, and then Gruber and I both pull Drygalski up, and nothing has ever felt better than these hands holding on to each other tightly. Tired from pulling ourselves and each other up, we lie on our backs and breathe deeply. The sky above us is grey, but so beautiful, particularly because we can feel the metal underneath us. It is still warm.

And then. The repeated One more time. The eternal

54 Once again. The parting of the eyelids. The intake of breath. The partial firing of the most essential and, for the moment, the only available areas of the brain. The sense of belonging to a species that is condemned to believe that belonging to this species makes it something special. Having to get up. Having to go on living. Wanting to go on living. Having to want to go on living. The fear of one day not being able to go on living. The first step. The force of gravity. The exhalation of carbon dioxide. The pointless knowledge of one's own existence wrapped like cotton wool around the world. The daily wonder at the existence of things.

Shall we go?
Yes.

55 It's still early in the morning. The sky is clear. We spot a vapour trail. Spot it when we're still amid the trees, through the widening gaps between the branches at the edge of the forest. We pick up our pace; the gaps grow wider. We step out of the forest, and right then, just as the full expanse of the sky is finally spread out above us again, with that line of white vapour right in the middle, slowly fraying at one end, we see before us an open field buried under a thin, pristine layer of snow.

Let's write something, says Drygalski. Maybe someone else will come along and see it.

And no one asks what they're supposed to do, this someone who may or may not come along. Whether they'll try to land, or drop a bomb, or a food crate, or whether they'll send a rescue team overland. We don't care. We're happy to have a plan, something to do, an idea leading to deliberate action and the vague recollection of the word 'sense' it brings with it, the associated language, letters perhaps, signs that we can write in the snow with our feet, stepping on that white, loose powder, down to the brown, frozen ground, and step by step, from our movements across the canvas of the field there emerges something that is strangely isolated from those movements. Each individual step is still meaningless, as is even the sequence of steps each of us takes. Only our communal choreography, born in our heads, agreed upon in advance and realised together in accordance with our synchronised conceptions, has the chance of attaining significance. A last dance, the single message that we leave behind for our saviours, for posterity, or for nothingness.

What should we write? 'Help'? In German or in English?
They're both a bit too intricate.
Plus: A cry for help might also attract the attention of someone who has no intention of helping.

How do you mean?

Well, you know. Whoever is responsible for all of this. Perhaps they'll see our message and come looking for us to finish the job.

We'd need to write something that will only mean something to someone with good intentions.

A cross?

Perhaps.

But what if the people on the plane are Muslims? Would they be inclined to help if they saw a cross?

Not all Muslims are radicals.

No. But imagine you were flying over a country that's been laid waste, and then down on the ground you see a crescent in the snow. And nothing else. Just a crescent. Would you help them?

Why a crescent?

But a cross signifies charity, doesn't it?

A cross is an instrument of torture.

All right.

What about a thumbs-up? Like on Facebook.

Do you 'like' this field?

Not particularly. But a thumbs-up implies, Hey, we're cool, we're OK, you can hang out with us, it might be

worth trying to get to know us.
But if you're flying over it?
Hmm.

We debate this a little while longer. We formulate sentences that would take weeks to write out on the field. We invent symbols that no one would understand. In the end, when we're close to giving up on the project as a whole, we decide to draw a massive peace sign.

In order to leave the white surface as intact as possible, we split up and approach the field from three different directions. Taking giant steps to leave only isolated dots in the snow, we establish a minimum distance from the field's edge. When we're ready, we signal to each other. Each of us turns to his right. And then we march. Taking short, firm steps, we stamp the last remnants of meaning onto the planet's surface. This is the message we will leave here. You can all go fuck yourselves. You can come here and kill us all if you want to, but first we're going to take this opportunity to write something in the hope that someone will read it and come and save us, and so we wish you all the best, the same thing we wish for ourselves: peace.

It's slow going. Veering gently to the left, we each trace a 120° arc toward the starting point of the one in front of us. Gruber is the first to reach his destination. Then me. We have to wait a few minutes for Drygalski to finish. I wonder whether he's really that much slower than the rest of us, or whether his section was actually longer. I loosen my scarf a little. The sun is already much higher in the sky. I hadn't noticed at all, having been focused on the snow directly in front of me which I was busy treading into the ground, but at last it's pleasantly warm now. The sun. The snow. Then Drygalski calls out, and we begin to march towards the centre of our circle. Circle of friends, I think to myself. And peace. And sun. And snow.

I take my hat off and stuff it in my pocket. I'm hot. I notice that the snow beneath my boots is growing thinner and wetter. Drygalski and Gruber are still over fifty metres away. I keep moving. When we finally meet in the middle we are all aware of the fact that in two hours at most there will be no visible trace left of our march for peace. Since none of us has any desire to say this out loud, we all stare at the sun in silence, until we are certain that we have all understood that the act of staring calmly at the sun while standing in a thawing field, in the middle of a rapidly dissolving message to posterity, can mean only one thing: You do all realise that snow tends to melt in the sun, right?

We don't bother finishing the peace sign by tracing the final line to the perimeter of the circle and instead simply leave the field. On the crest of the next hill, as we are about to re-enter the forest, we turn around one last time.

The best or nothing, says Gruber.

Drygalski furrows his brow, but seems not to dare ask Gruber what he means. Behind us lies a gigantic Mercedes-Benz logo.

56 And then we can't find anything to eat, two days in a row. And so we eat the fruits of the forest, or at least what we city boys take to be the fruits of the forest. Quite apart from the fact that not much grows in the forest in early April, we also have no idea whether the things that do grow are even edible. We don't even really know what edible means, exactly, since there is a lot you can put in your mouth, chew, and swallow. We walk through the forest, our stomachs nothing but gaping holes through which the pain creeps in, slowly making its way upwards to our throats, our heads, our eyes. Everything you look at hurts, but you keep looking because you have to look closely, you have to know whether this is something you could potentially put in your mouth, chew, and swallow. And you notice yourself growing less and less discerning with each new thing you examine. Of course you used to

have clearly defined ideas about what you would put into your body, which substances and compounds you would feed it, and of course you used to think about the way the things you put in your body are the things that build you, repair you, rework and adapt you – so don't eat too much junk.

We walk through the forest. It is our only, our last friend, and our eyes dart from one thing to the next, and Drygalski says, There should really be a big political campaign to ensure that nothing like this ever happens again. People have to know what it means to live in peace, in Europe, in a harmless state of boredom. And he looks right through me as he shouts, for the first time since I've known him he shouts, shouts at me, and he shouts: Do you know? Do you understand? And all the while he is staring straight through me at the barren undergrowth behind me.

Gruber is tugging at a root and says, You know, I'm a normal guy, I'm interested in women, and I believe in goodness, which is why I pursue my interest in women in a reserved, polite manner. And then the root slips through his hand and suddenly he's sitting in the mud, his hands bloody, and he says, If you had to choose would you rather fuck another man in the arse or be fucked in the arse by another man? You've got to help yourself, he says, that's part of being human. Who would we be if we stopped doing that? Can I help you? Look, there are some deciduous trees over there. Deciduous trees are better than evergreens. Leaves don't hurt the way pine needles do. Should I go and get some leaves for one of you. There are leaves there, nice, soft leaves, he says. But the trees are still bare.

Drygalski is sitting cross-legged under a spruce pulling the scales off a pine cone, examining each one carefully from all sides, holding them against the light, before throwing them over his shoulder saying, No, that's no good, that's not right, that's not it.

I move away from them a little. I go deeper into the forest, and I hear Drygalski calling, A political community strong enough to keep the peace, and national identity can't play a role at all, and economic interests may be a primitive reason but a practical one – no moral code is as powerful as your bank account and your stomach. And Gruber shouts, The disproportion between the infinite emptiness of space and the finitude of things is the reason for the boundless superiority of the female sex! The vagina will always be bigger than the penis! And then his words become unclear, I think he is now pulling on a root with his teeth, and I go a little farther away. I pass more trees. And as I pass them, I touch them with my fingers, gently at first, but then something changes – not my pace or the length of my stride, all that remains constant – but my fingers begin to touch the trees more firmly, start to try to grasp them, at first just my finger-tips, then my nails, and I can hear my nails scratching the bark, and the scratching grows louder with every tree I pass and the tension begins to increase in my fingers, in my arms, in my shoulders. My nails dig deeper into the bark of every tree I pass, and I keep going because I don't want any of this, but the bark is getting caught under my fingernails, my hands want to hold on to that bark because it is there, it is just so there, so present, it is, is something, and I need something inside me right now and I keep going and then the nail on my ring finger on my right hand breaks, and it's just a fingernail but it makes me so unbelievably angry and sad and I stumble and then I'm crying. Tears are streaming down my face. I'm crying for my broken fingernail, and then I fall down into the soft, decomposing pine needles, hitting them first with my knees, then my hands, then the rest of me, and ever so slowly I press my face into the cool, damp, mouldy materiality of the forest floor. My mouth is wide open, the ground comes closer, closer and closer, and the needles are moving in my mouth, and in the needles something else is moving too, and I think, ants, perhaps, and then I pass out.

57

When I wake up it is raining again. We are sitting in a circle. We are eating. We are eating pine needles. We are eating shoots. We are eating bark. We are eating roots. In very small portions, of course. We don't want to put excessive strain on our bodies. An hour later Gruber and I both have diarrhoea; Drygalski is throwing up. We're not sure who's better off. We are lying on the forest floor and ascertain that we are still alive. Somehow we manage to get up. We lean on the trees and each other, swaying through the forest. We want to get out of this perpetual gloom, this green, this grey. At some point there are fewer trees, spaced farther apart, not as tall: the edge of the forest. A field. The rain can no longer be ignored.

Spring is in the air, says Gruber.

The last patches of white are slowly dissolving on the plain before us. The sky is empty and grey, and if it weren't for the rain you would not have suspected that the temperature was above freezing. We can see stones, meadows, fields, tree stumps, the ruins of walls. We see the world in all its indifferent, unadorned thereness. We step out into the rain. Getting wet wakes us all up for a brief moment, we feel more alive even though getting wet is always followed by a near-freezing to death in the night. We go out into the rain through the open field. At the boundary between two fallow fields there stands an old linden tree. That's our goal. The ground is sodden, the mud sticking heavily to our boots. We raise them up like children's heads and plunge them back into the dark brown mud, our hair streaked across our faces, the rain forming droplets on our greasy foreheads and running down our chins and necks, down our backs and onto our chests. The linden tree between the fields looks inviting, that's where we want to go, we have to get there right away; after all, it's raining, and even though we were sheltered in the forest which is now behind us but still closer than the linden tree, we carry on through the field, towards the tree, in the damp, grey air.

At some point we reach it, and we lie down beneath the delicate young leaves and the rain doesn't reach us as much and then it's already getting dark again. Did we really take that long to get across the fields? Perhaps it's just clouds. It doesn't matter. We lie down and we know that, if we wake up tomorrow morning at all, we will wake up early, because it seems appropriate in this situation, abandoned or burnt-down villages, or burnt bodies, dissolving human beings, fog, soot, death. It feels appropriate to get up early when you are fighting for survival. And so we will get up early tomorrow morning as well, but when we're awake we will once again see that there is precious little we can do to contribute to our own survival. We will see that we are still here. That will be all. There will be nothing for us to do. If we find some wood, we will make a fire. If not, we won't. Then we will try to keep warm by jumping from one foot to the other, doing squats and carefully rotating our stiff hips. It's been a long time since we had the strength for press-ups.

58

Before drifting off, I see the light green of the first linden leaves above me, how it merges with the brown of the branches and the trunk and with the thin layer of water running down the whole of it, until it all merges with the grey sky. The world becomes a fog descending upon not only the things out there but also the words inside me.

As I doze, I see Gruber. He is walking with his head held straight. With each step he places his foot carefully on the ground, lifting the other a bit higher than necessary. He is leaning slightly backward, and after each step he pauses for a moment, as if incredulous that the road hasn't crumbled into the earth, that the tectonic plate beneath it is still intact.

As I doze, I see Gruber as he was a few weeks ago, in

the warehouse, staring at fifteen thousand pairs of men's double-stitched Y-fronts, 30% cotton, 70% polyester, packed neatly into boxes and carefully stacked on EUR pallets. They are ready. Each easy-open packet contains five pairs, the Italian design and trendy blue-and-red colours visible through the clear plastic window on the front. Gruber's eyes scan the packing slips bearing the addresses of the wholesalers awaiting this shipment of men's undergarments, and he imagines the fifteen thousand penises which will soon be resting securely in them, occasionally being manoeuvred through the opening in the front and then put away again, and he imagines the thirty thousand testicles that will remain patiently in place all the while, comfortably couched in the cotton-polyester blend. He looks at the pallets and imagines the billions upon billions of spermatozoa being produced every day by those testicles in those Y-fronts, and he imagines the thousands of human beings who may or may not be born as a result, and the houses they will build and the cars they will drive, the women they will love, and the IT solutions, household objects, commodities certificates, hit songs and men's undergarments these people will produce, some time, perhaps.

Gruber is waiting for the DPD guy. The boxes are packed, the forms have been filled in, he's had more than enough coffee, and the others have all gone off for lunch. He goes back to his office, sits down at his computer, opens his browser and types the word 'facial' into the search function on RedTube. He's not thinking of masturbating, that would be pathetic, masturbating at work, he's not a teenage boy any more, and besides the company belongs to his uncle, no, probably he won't even get an erection right away, and he clicks on Tera Patrick vs. Rocco Siffredi & Nacho Vidal, not because he wants to wank, but because he enjoys seeing sperm land on a lovely face, in a lovely mouth, on a lovely tongue. Lovely sperm from a lovely cock.

The telephone rings.

Pro-Fashion, Gruber speaking.

On his screen, three naked figures by the pool.

Not at lunch, Herr Gruber?

The progress bar is growing.

Herr Özbay! Where are you?

The three figures begin to move. The video freezes for a moment.

Brunnthal junction. It'll be a while.

You do know that the shipment has to be delivered to head office in Penzberg today, right?

The video resumes.

What do you want me to do?

Nacho gives Tera a slap in the face, his little silver bracelet glinting in the sun.

No idea. Listen to the traffic alerts?

Then he sticks his thick member in her mouth.

Herr Gruber. I'm sorry. There was no way I could have predicted this.

Rocco approaches from behind. His cock is even thicker than Nacho's. He lays it gently on Tera's fontanelle and begins to gyrate his hips, as if he wants to inseminate her scalp. Unperturbed, she carries on sucking Nacho's cock, like she hasn't had anything to eat for weeks. Her large hoop earrings swing back and forth.

Granted. So what now?

Well, you know the people at Metro's dispatch office.

Rocco takes his penis out of Tera's hair.

So?

Rocco strokes his cock a little. Evidently the little number with the scalp wasn't as much of a turn-on as his passionate expression might have led one to believe.

It's all just an act, after all.

I thought maybe you could persuade them to stay a little longer today.

Rocco goes around to stand in front of Tera next to Nacho.

Are you serious?

He gently slaps her cheek with his now fully engorged member.

Well, you know.

Side by side like this, even Nacho cuts a rather poor figure compared to Rocco.

So: you are late. You probably won't be able to make the delivery on time. As a result, my company will probably demand compensation from you. And in order to avoid that, you want me to call the Penzberg people?

Rocco is not just your average joe.

Look, if we don't deliver today, then it will above all be *you* who fail to deliver. Metro don't give a shit whether it's the driver's fault or not.

Tera can barely fit it in her mouth.

Is that a threat?

But somehow she manages it. Nacho wipes some pre-cum on her cheek, but he seems to sense that he is superfluous here now.

Herr Gruber. How long have we been working together?

Oh, Tera, the indignities you put up with.

All right. You've almost moved me to tears. But why don't you call them yourself?

Tera, you beautiful creature.

Are you really asking me?

Tera, with your big, dark eyes.

Absolutely.

Tera, with your long, black hair.

What do you think the Penzbergers are going to do when I call and say, Hello, this is Özbay?

Ah.

Gruber presses pause.

I'm sorry. What was I thinking?

Five years we've been working together.

I'm really sorry.

It's OK.

All right, we'll figure it out. I'll call those Nazis at Metro and you just race to get here, all right?

Did you say race?

I mean hurry!

Thank you, Herr Gruber.

No problem. We'll get this sorted out. We always have in the past.

See you later.

As I doze, I see Gruber press play again.

59

In the end, we don't wake up until quite late. Maybe because we're starving to death. Maybe because we've been walking ever so slightly uphill for the past several days, the upward slope almost imperceptible, so you end up walking faster than you really can, and you get more tired than you should, because you think to yourself, this isn't steep, and so you don't stop to rest. And at some point you're puking up bile, because there's nothing else in your stomach.

We leave the linden tree and the field behind us and plunge back into the forest on the far side. It is a thick, dark forest, it is wet and muddy and hard to walk through, and when, in the middle of all that green, we suddenly come across an empty motorway, it comes as a shock. We follow it north, it's good to be walking on tarmac again, and a few hours later we spot a couple of buildings with a long flat roof projecting out over the motorway, nothing underneath it apart from a few small metal-and-glass booths at regular intervals, one for each lane of the motorway.

Gruber says: There, the border.
Drygalski says: Something's not right.

I imagine that if, after us, someone rebuilds the world, it will be a silent world. People will only exchange glances, careful gestures and gentle touches, and they will use their vocal cords only for laughing or sighing. People will point to the things they mean, and anything that you can't point to – either because it isn't there or because it's an abstract concept – you simply won't be able to mean any longer. And so people will keep silent, day by day, year by year, until not even the faintest memory will remain of the ancient custom of using the mouth and the tongue to give form to the sounds the human body can produce, of dividing them up – articulating them – and of studying and classifying the individual parts, dividing them into ever smaller units, and then of inscribing the signs that supposedly correspond to these smallest possible units, on stone, or on silicon, or on paper. And all knowledge of these skills will disappear for ever, gradually and irrevocably, expelled like air from the lungs, and with it this immense realm of bodiless propositions will also disappear, this alien, transparent world that is language, this sea of ghosts.

And so no one will ever again be able to say the words Nation, or You or I, or Love, or I'm afraid I don't love you any more, or Economic equality, or We would like to welcome you aboard this Boeing 737 aircraft travelling to Frankfurt am Main, or Why have they not torn down the border between Germany and Austria by now? We've been in Schengen for more than twenty years, or Better safe than sorry, or If push came to shove it would be relatively easy to get a site like this operational again, or Depending on how you look at it, or Wait a minute, or What happened here?, or Burning tyres atop barricades of cars and debris, or Breached barbed wire fences, or Dead soldiers in unmarked uniforms, or A path right through the middle, cleared by the bulldozer ploughing right through the rubbish and the people, or Why is the bulldozer on the other side lying on its side?, or How can something that broad tip over like that?, or The crater next to it in the tarmac, or Its tracks are broken, or Of course we're moving along as fast as we can, what else are we supposed to do? We want to get out of here, but we don't want to go back, so we have got to go through there, boys, or Some people are always quicker than the others, or It isn't me or Drygalski, or Somehow I've got a bad feeling about this, or Then of course at that exact moment there's a yellow flash, or Noise, a physically palpable noise, or Wind, a gale that knocks you to the ground without warning and then kicks you a few times for good measure, or Blood, empty skin, entrails and pulverised bones, or Teeth, a friend's teeth that are suddenly stuck to the outside of your own cheek, or Gruber, or What exactly is the difference between an anti-tank mine and an anti-personnel mine?

And a few generations later, people will once more live as molecular aggregates equal to other molecular aggregates, things among other things. They will be quick trees with eyes, or slow, soft stones with hair.

I stay on the ground for a little while. My ears feel

as though they have sealed themselves of their own accord, hermetically, each one trapping a wasp inside. I postpone opening my eyes for the time being. The smell of wet tarmac. There are small stones lodged in my forehead.

Drygalski, I shout, but I can't hear a thing, except the angry buzzing in my head. I can distinctly feel the movements my mouth is making, which to me have to do with his name, but I am no longer certain what it is that I am saying, if I am even saying anything at all. I open my eyes. They seem to be working. Carefully, I raise my head. I turn it to the left. I can see chunks of tarmac, shreds of clothing, of Gruber. I can see Drygalski. He is still there. He is lying on his side, and I can see his face, and can I see that his mouth is moving. I have no idea what he is saying.

60

Walking together as a pair is something completely different from walking together as a group. The other's position is clearly defined, as, by implication, is one's own. The Others don't exist any more, there is no longer the illusion of different individuals who all need to be treated differently. There is only the singular Other, the singular Not Me. There is only a singular You.

Do you remember that time we found Gruber's father's air rifle in the basement and went and shot eggs in the hallway? How we called for each other and we all came, and then we shot and shot and were all excited. The rifle had a cherrywood stock, and the greased barrel shone in the light from the halogen spots.

And then we ran out of eggs but still had a lot of

ammunition, so we all got into Fürst's old Mazda, he'd just got his licence, and by then it was dark, and you shouted, Drive-by, baby!, and we drove off, three of us on the back seat holding the rifle, and Golde and Fürst were in the front, and we listened to NWA's 'Approach to Danger' and whistled along to the sine wave.

We took a later turning out of the city in order not to arouse suspicions and then we were on the right side of the B304 and we were going exactly 61 km/h, just over the speed limit, and there was hardly any traffic because it was a week night, summer holiday, and then we could finally see the Upper Bavarian Horticultural Show grounds up ahead, and we saw the tents and combine harvesters and tractors and it was all empty and quiet, protected by a tall fence, and we got closer and closer and we could see the giant inflatable elephant – what is an elephant doing at a garden show anyway? – and we put a pellet right between its eyes.

Or maybe not between the eyes, maybe it was behind one ear, or in the stomach, but we definitely hit it, I mean it was huge, and we weren't complete idiots, and

Fürst and Golde both distinctly heard the impact, and so did I.

The fucking thing just stood there as if nothing had happened, but we had to get going, we didn't have the nerve for a second drive-by, supposedly there were security guards there, so we drove back to Gruber's house, parked the car and got our bikes and rode back again, this time with Gruber's combat knife, just you and me, the others couldn't be bothered, they wanted to watch some horror film, but we went back there to finish that fucking beast off.

We hid our bikes in the bushes and climbed the fence, and we could hear the elephant just whistling faintly as we skulked in the shadows from tent to tent, like special forces on a mission in Kandahar. It was just whistling faintly when we realised that there probably weren't any security guards, why should there be?, and it kept whistling faintly even when we rammed the blade into the thing, once, twice, three times, after nothing had happened the first time because you had forgotten to take the leather sheath off, but even then nothing happened, it just whistled a little more, and then all you could hear was the hum of the giant compressor pumping air into the elephant, more air than could escape through the tiny holes we were able to make, and so we rode back and never mentioned it again. And the others were tactful enough never to ask us about it either.

Yes, I remember.

61

We are heading for a mountain, and the mountain has a hole in it. Right in the spot we are heading for, they have dynamited the rock. The hole is round and walled with stones. A short distance into the hole, the road, which outside is covered in mud and broken stones, suddenly regains its original smooth surface; there is even a dashed white line, here, just past the entrance, before it disappears into the darkness inside the mountain. The entrance has a museum-like quality to it, recalling an order within which one could move about freely, even through solid rock if need be. As we step out of the grey light and the cold wind and the incomprehensible circumstances and into this tunnel everything becomes calmer, clearer, smaller. Our footfalls once again make a sound that clearly distinguishes each contact between foot and ground from the next, no more scuffing through gravel, no more wading through mud, no more trudging through snow. We are walking, our feet on solid ground, and suddenly we realise that we are wearing boots and clothes and hold our heads high, feeling civilised, as we march deeper into the blackness.

The time it takes for our eyes to adjust to the darkness grows longer the less light there is, and when our eyes can no longer keep up with our feet we stop as if on command.

What if we can't go on? What if the tunnel is blocked and there's no way through?
Then we will turn around.

There are no objections or better suggestions. And so we start moving again, slowly, holding our hands out in front of our bodies, pathetic little breakwaters in the blackness, stepping carefully, feeling for solid ground, in case there's a rock, or a corpse, or a hole in the ground.

I imagine every logically possible obstacle, arranged

in order of the likelihood of their occurrence in a tunnel in the alpine upland following the total collapse of organised society: cars, intact, abandoned; cars, burnt-out shells; lorries, intact or burnt out; military vehicles, armoured personnel carriers; busloads of refugees; lorryloads of food for cut-off areas; motorcycles, bicycles, pedestrians, hundreds, thousands, intact, left behind, burnt. Aeroplanes, helicopters, hidden away for a covert counter-strike; secret stockpiles of ordnance and small arms, secured by anti-personnel mines, anti-tank barriers, barbed wire; depots full of food, chemical weapons or cultural heritage to be preserved for posterity; bunkers where people have found refuge, men, women and children; or perhaps just women, a private brothel for some regional separatist army; or perhaps the final batch of beer brewed by the Ducal Bavarian Brewery, Tegernsee.

We start walking faster, our arms no longer stretched out in front of us. We walk on, the air stands still in here, the echoes of our footfalls are nice and clear, the ground is still solid, the world before us is black. We are not afraid of it. But then at some point we begin to slow down again, until only one of is still moving and soon thereafter neither of us is, and then there is complete silence.

We can hear each other's breathing as we stare intently into the blackness in front of us, so close it burns our eyes. We look around. Behind us there is only the faintest glimmer, impossibly far away, a memory of the fact that we came into this tunnel at one point, and this memory looks very fragile, and we are afraid that it will disappear if we take so much as a single step farther.

Don't you think we'd better turn around?
Yes.

We turn around. And with each passing metre on the way to the entrance, or exit, our steps grow faster and more confident, we know the way, we have a goal, it feels good, and when the greyness ahead of us begins to look truly grey and there are only two or three hundred metres between us and it, we break into a run, we run and run until finally we are back out in the wind, happy to know where we are and where we are not, we are standing out in the wind and we can see mud and trees and sky and for a few minutes we are just happy and cold, happy and cold.

62

On our way back we give the border crossing a wide berth. We stay in the forest as much as possible. In an abandoned hunting lodge we discover eight tins of ravioli and an olive green cagoule. On the first day we take turns wearing it, switching every thousand paces, with the result that that night we are both just as wet as if we had never found the thing. That evening we decide only to swap once per day, each morning, regardless of the weather. We draw straws to determine who gets to wear it first. I win.

Every day we eat one tin, cracking it open on a rock, licking any spilt sauce off the ground and then taking turns slowly eating one raviolo at a time, until we finish the tin. Drygalski's jacket pockets are big enough to hold one tin each, mine are not. I loosen my belt and stuff them down the back of my trousers. The chafing sores have stopped weeping by the time we finish the last tin.

We'll be there soon, says Drygalski.
Yes, I say.

I'm looking forward to returning to the last place where everything was still good. Perhaps we should just have stayed there. Perhaps we never should have looked down into the valley.

63 When we get to the cabin we can see right away that someone has been there. The door is open. We definitely closed it, and whoever has been or still is in there and who hasn't closed the front door is definitely not one of us, nobody we know, since we know Gruber's father and he won't stand for doors being left open. We do not slow our pace, our hearts do not beat faster than they are already beating from the ascent, we simply keep heading for the cabin, even though we know that there might still be someone in there, someone who may want to kill us. We make a slight detour via the shed where Gruber's father keeps the tools for clearing snow and chopping wood.

The man is asleep. We stand there, looking at him. He is lying on his back. We can see his chest rise and fall, his face is turned to one side, into the pillow he is clutching with his right hand. I am clutching a shovel, Drygalski an axe. Our breathing slows to match that of the sleeper. We look at him. It's been a long time since we've seen someone sleeping who isn't one of us, or breathing, and I think to myself, what a fantastic invention the heart is, 36 million beats per year, times 82.7 for the average European, all by itself. The only thing you have to do is eat, drink and breathe.

His clothes are similar to ours. He is roughly the same age as we are. His skin is a similar colour to ours, as is his hair. Similar height, insofar as you can tell when someone is lying down. We can't see his eyes. I ask myself when I should put the shovel down, lean it against the bed, or the wall, when Drygalski will put down the axe, when we will put the tools back in the shed where they were, where they belong. I watch this man breathe, he is breathing more calmly than me, more slowly, peacefully. He seems content. I can feel the cold, smooth wood in my hands, the weight of the steel blade in my left. I don't know whether Drygalski is waiting for me to put down the shovel, or whether I'm waiting for him to put down the axe. All I know is that I keep holding the shovel, it's not heavy, the wood is smooth, the curvature is perfect. The edges of the rust-coloured blade are marked by silver scratches from hacking away at the ice on the stone steps leading down to the road. The man stops breathing. I tighten my grip on the shovel. He opens his eyes. I am holding the shovel tightly. He doesn't look at us; he stares into the pillow. Drygalski shifts his weight to his other foot. Then the man leaps out of bed.

I don't know whether things would have gone differently if he hadn't got up. I don't know whether he should have tried talking to us. I have no idea which changes to the past might have produced which changes to the present, any more than I have any idea about the future.

He jumps up and lunges away from the bed, ramming his shoulder into Drygalski's stomach, knocking him off his feet, and perhaps I wouldn't have gone after him if Drygalski hadn't fallen over or if he hadn't got back on his feet so fast. I manage to raise my arm before my head collides with the door the man has slammed behind him. I throw the door back open in time to see him at the end of the corridor bolting for the whiteness outside the cabin. I hear Drygalski's footsteps behind me, he's running fast, faster than me, so I run faster as well, and then we are already on the slope and we can see the man ten, twenty metres ahead of us, making his way diagonally upward through the snow. Every three paces he slips and falls and gets back up. So do we. The distance remains the same. We are running as fast as we can, and so is he, I assume. He is slow, but so are we. We are carrying a shovel and an axe. We gain on him. I am beginning to think we can catch him, and I am amazed; after all, there's only one of him and two of us and we are getting in each other's way, overtaking each other, perhaps that's why we're that little bit faster. I have the distinct impression that the distance is shrinking, and I'm not sure whether I think that's good or bad. I am running through wet snow up the side of a mountain in pursuit of a man and I am gaining on him. Why would I stop now?

When we're still three metres away he falls down, just shy of the young fir trees by the stream, and this time he's not getting back up, and we don't stop or slow down, we keep running, getting closer and closer, and then for the first time I am looking him straight in the eye and I am still busy wondering what human qualities you can possibly discern from someone's eyes when our fists go out in front of us, automatically, as the logical continuation of our motion, the motion of pursuit, no more and no less, the pursuit of nothing in particular except of course happiness, change, of a life that is somehow different from this one, and in our fists are our weapons – tools which you could use to build houses, to make chairs and tables where you could sit and enjoy meals or establish universal systems of value – and our fists holding these weapons land in the middle of his face, on his pale cheeks, his forehead, in the gaping holes that have suddenly opened up, merging at first with his wide-open eyes and then coming together to form a single dark abyss at the bottom of which lies the single, definitive grey that unites us all, until that too is broken down and carried off by the flies and the ants, fed to larvae, digested and excreted. So this is what a brain looks like.

I'm glad Drygalski hit him just as hard as I did and just as often. I'm glad he's not saying anything. We stand and inspect our handiwork for a while. The dark halo around what's left of the man's head is spreading astonishingly quickly, and I take a deep breath, feeling the cold air in my lungs, and as I do so I am thinking one single thought, for the first time in a long while: it is better to be alive.

I don't know whether it's been one minute or ten. I see Drygalski fall to his knees and with his left hand begin clearing away the wet, slushy snow beside the man's smashed head until the damp, flattened ground comes into view, and then he begins to hack at it with his axe, once, twice, three times, four times. Drygalski is hacking at the ground and I am ashamed because for a moment I have no idea why. What the hell is he doing? But then I realise, thank God, I realise just in time to avoid looking like an idiot in front of my last living friend. I know that this is the only right thing to do, the rightest thing we've done since we saw that village in flames, perhaps even in our entire lives, and then I sink the shovel into the earth that Drygalski has loosened with his axe. I pick up the first load of earth and place it carefully to one side. We will need it later.

By the time we deposit the last shovelful of earth over the man's body it is almost dark. We don't have the energy to pat the grave flat. We are breathing heavily. We lean on each other, making sure not to hold onto each other for longer than our exhaustion requires. Then we stand there for a while, each of us on his own, by that rectangle of brown framed with dirty snow. We look into the valley. The bare peaks on the opposite side are still clearly visible. Down below it is already night.

64

I imagine Drygalski, a few weeks ago, in his laboratory, searching for his cure for cancer.

In his latex-clad hand he is holding a Petri dish with razor-thin slices of frozen mouse tumours.

His red Air Max IIs are planted firmly on the ground.

The day before he benched a hundred kilos for the first time.

The formaldehyde stains on his lab coat are not visible to the naked eye.

His mother is also his boss here. Technically it's his father who runs things – he owns the lab – but he never asks how work was when Drygalski comes home to the house that he still shares with his parents. His mother is at the lab today too. She is about twenty metres away, past the decontamination tunnel, behind a large monitor, and while his mother is going over project descriptions and updating employee files perhaps she

is thinking about the expensive equipment that her son
is using back here.

He thinks, Her son. He thinks, This expensive equipment
I'm using. He thinks, All non-bonded or non-specifically
bonded molecular probes have to be eluted before the
samples are placed under the fluorescence microscope.
He thinks, I hope I can do it this time.

He can see his own reflection in the glass cabinet next
to the microscope, and he can see that he cannot see any
part of himself except for the white overall with a hood,
mask and safety specs.

He has the correct sequence of steps in his head. He
could have recited the correct sequence in his sleep, if
you had woken him up, let's say at three in the morning,
which fortunately has never occurred. He is single, but
at least he sleeps well, and his single status will change
once he moves out of his parents' house, he just needs
to work some more, save up some money so he can buy
a flat and get out of there.

It'll be some house-warming.

He can even recite the correct sequence of steps after
five vodka tonics.

There'll be some chick, a friend of someone's girlfriend's,

who'll feel right at home and stay the night.

He can recite them after ten vodka tonics.

Sometimes we ask him what the steps are. He never tells us.

The monitor lights up.

The image is complete.

Shit. Back to square one.

65

We say less and less to each other. One-word sentences give way to sullen grunts and half-hearted gestures. Gradually we even stop looking each other in the eye. We communicate sideways. There is someone beside you. He can also see that there is nothing down there in the valley, he is also clearing away some of the mud from the entrance, he can also see that the bread is covered in mould, and: he is also hungry. He also used to call the central area of this building the living room, the stove the stove, the firewood firewood, or at least he did when there was still some left, the chair the chair, the table the table, the floor the floor, and the lady with the sword in her heart on the poster above the couch Mary, Mother of God. As long as there is someone beside you, everything is still in its right place.

At some point the last slice of mouldy bread has been eaten. The snow is melting. The patches of green on the slopes seem fake and unhealthy to us. A uniform white would be nicer. White would be more appropriate for a day like today. We are sitting in the living room, waiting, and sitting, and then it gets dark, and we keep waiting. We sit in the dark and wait for it to be over.

Snow or no snow. Light or no light. Lying or sitting or standing, or in fact probably lying, that's probably best when there's nothing to do apart from standing and sitting and nothing to see apart from snow or no snow, light or no light.

66 At dawn it begins to snow again. I see Drygalski gripping the edge of the table with his fingers. He lets go. Then he grips it again. His eyes are closed. I pretend not to notice him. I am lying on the bench, keeping my eyes closed as well, and only occasionally peering in his direction through a narrow slit in my eyelids. Outside the windows the dark green slopes are slowly turning white again. Drygalski places his other hand on the seat of his chair and grips it. His knuckles are as white as the snow on the windowsill. He pushes himself up, slowly extends one leg and lowers his chin slowly to his chest, leans his torso forward, his centre of gravity shifting above his hips, over the edge of the chair, over his knees, and just before he tips over and falls face first on the floor he lifts his buttocks and is standing. Carefully he stretches his legs. Slowly, he staggers over to the sideboard. He takes a small knife

from the knife block. I know that the small knives are the sharpest, I occasionally used to use one of them to chop onions. Drygalski pauses in front of the door and looks over at me. I can feel his gaze even though my eyes are still closed to the extent that I can discern shapes, objects and colours, but not pupils. Drygalski is looking at me, something he has rarely done recently. He is standing there with the small knife in one hand, his other hand on the handle of the door that leads into the corridor. His back is bent, when it always used to be straight, and the way his trousers are hanging around his legs and his jacket over his shoulders, you would never have suspected that Drygalski used to be overweight. I can just about see the dark circles around his eyes. Holes inside which, somewhere, lies that which I used to know, if it is even still there. I will never find out. I'm not really looking. I'm keeping my eyes half closed. When he takes his hand off the handle and raises it, slowly, solemnly, as if he were about to give a speech, I open my eyes, but before Drygalski can notice, he changes his mind, puts his hand back on the door handle, opens the door and is gone.

67 Do you remember, it was four o'clock in the morning, at your going-away party at my place. There were still people there but all the guests had left, because the ones who remained were much more than guests, and we were jumping up and down in a circle in the living room, our arms interlocked around the shoulders of the ones on either side of us. We were kicking the air in between us in time with the music, as if we were trying to destroy anything that could separate us, like a football team after a victory, a football team who are their own biggest and only fans, and we were dancing and kicking the air, the music was really loud and we didn't care what it was, and then you said, I've really got to go now, and then we opened the circle, we let you out, and you pulled us in one by one, we hugged, and slapped you on the back, Good luck, Take care, Have fun, and then you walked out of the living room and

we went back to our drunken footballers' dance, and then you came back in one more time and we all gave you another hug and patted you on the back again and said, Take care, and Have fun, and then you left and came back a third time, and we all burst out laughing, Go on, bugger off on your stupid round-the-world trip!, and you were laughing too, and then I saw you from behind in the corridor heading for the door and then you were gone, and six months later you came back in one piece and we acted like nothing had happened. Do you remember, Drygalski? Drygalski. I said, do you remember?

68

Walking through the snow on the mountainside is hard enough when you're well fed and don't have arthritis or frostbitten toes or pressure sores on your behind. I spot the round, red stain from far away. Drygalski is lying there face down on the ground. The knife to his right, besides his open hand. His left arm by his side. He is lying with his head pointing in the direction of the valley. He's done that so that he would bleed out more quickly. I kneel beside him and touch the back of his neck. He's barely warm. I see how thin he is. I run my hand down his back, I can feel his bony shoulder blades, his spine, his pelvis. I can feel that he no longer has a fat arse.

I see what Drygalski must have seen as he stepped outside in the knowledge that this would be the last time he would step outside and see anything. The grey sky. The valley. The burnt-down village. The treeline on the mountains opposite, a straight, dark boundary, below which all is dark, and above which the peaks rise up, dissolving into the sky. I imagine Drygalski standing there, looking at all of this one last time, at this one, never-changing, frozen world. He takes a few steps out into the field, onto the slope, he kneels down and feels for his carotid artery with his left hand, then he sinks the knife into it with his right, calmly, deliberately, hard. Then he puts down the knife and gently allows himself to fall forward, and as his body falls over, so too does his knowledge of the world, of up and down, right and wrong, of the names of the things all around him, all of that falls with him towards the valley, and it flows with his blood down the mountain, downward towards the centre of the Earth.

I would have done the same for you, I think, picking up the knife with my right hand and hitching Drygalski's jacket up with my left. Each one of us would have done the same thing for all the others, I think, pushing his jumper up. We were the only ones left, I think, pulling his jeans down over his emaciated arse, without even loosening his belt. You beat me to it, I think. His buttocks are as white as the snow. The blade pushes against the cold skin, pushes deep and then the tissue rips and the flesh expands, enveloping the steel. Blood seeps out. With a careful sawing motion, I trace the outline of a square. Then I remove it.

69

If there should ever be another perfectly ordinary Monday, in November for all I care, when my alarm goes off at six thirty a.m. I will leap out of bed like the St Petersburg ballet. I will stand bold upright in the dark listening to that rhythmical beeping, I will move my head in time, up and down, then left and right, harder and harder, and tears of joy will fly from my eyes in all directions, in the morning darkness.

I will lie down flat on the floor and crawl like a seal across the groaning parquet towards the bathroom, naked, and I will hope to get a splinter of oak, oiled, antique, which will let me know that this is all real.

With feigned nonchalance I will get in the shower, turn the tap and scream as though the water were ice cold, but it will be hot, wonderfully hot, and I will scream anyway in disbelief at belonging to a species that was capable of designing and building such an apparatus.

I will resolve not to leave the shower for three whole days.

The skin on my fingers will become wrinkled.

After half an hour I will get out of the shower after all and I will take a freshly washed flannel, smelling of fabric softener, and run it under ice-cold water, and then I will stuff it in my mouth and then I will take a large bath towel into the living room and spread it out on the shag rug, and then I will lie down on it and roll myself up inside the rug and the towel.

I will revel in the sound the flannel makes when I suck on it and in the cold water emitted by the cotton fabric directly into my mouth.

Then I will go back into the bathroom.

I will put moisturising cream in the palm of my hand and then slap myself in the face with it, first one cheek, then the other.

I will run into the bedroom as fast as I can, my head only barely missing the door frame, and I will smash through the mirrored sliding door of my wardrobe and dive with the wreckage right into the hard shelves full of soft textiles so that I, the shelves and the fabrics crash onto the floor, and then I will writhe my way into my clothes like a snake.

Whatever is still clinging to my body when I exit the wardrobe I will declare my favourite outfit.
I will leave the house and wait for the sunrise.

It will be a clear day.

And when the sun appears I will inhale the cool, fresh air and say: Sun.

Then I will smile. I will do this every morning.

And after just a couple of years it will be impossible for an outside observer to determine whether it is the sun that brings forth the word or the word that brings forth the sun.

AUTHOR'S ACKNOWLEDGEMENTS

I would like to thank the Swiss Arts Council Pro Helvetia, the Canton of Bern and the City of Biel/Bienne for their support for the writing of this novel.

Thanks also to Julia Weber, Hansjörg Schertenleib, Silvio Huonder, Paul Brodowsky, Matthias Nawrat, Philipp Mattheis, Robert Kumsta, Godehard Brüntrup and my Stammtisch.